Valley of the Shadow

Valley of the Shadow

by Christopher Davis

St. Martin's Press
New York

Design by Jean Wisenbaugh

Library of Congress Cataloging-in-Publication Data

Davis, Christopher.
    Valley of the shadow.
    I. Title.
PS3554.A9329V35 1988   813'.54   88-1936
ISBN 0-312-01843-6

First Edition
10 9 8 7 6 5 4 3 2 1

Acknowledgments

This book started as a short story and would have remained one without the advice of my editor, Michael Denneny, and it would not have been written at all without the understanding and support of my lover, Mark Blasius. My thanks and gratitude to them both.

Additionally, I must thank the many people who read this as a manuscript or who encouraged me while it was being written, among them Olivia Joyner, Lenny Tropp, Carolyn Francis, Virginia Washington, Asja Cronin, Franklin Mitchell, and Natalie Hurst, and Barbara Zappavigna for giving me the time to complete it.

Finally, I must, as always, thank my dear friend Michael O., who, over the years, has had the patience to read almost everything I have written and comment wisely on it.

Valley of
the Shadow

Chapter *I*

I can remember when I was young, not very young, not an infant as some people claim to remember, but still young, when my body was weak and small. I remember my father teaching me how to swim. I was afraid of the water when I was young and small and I remember my father taking me out into it and holding me under my stomach and then letting me go. I

cannot remember any more than that: I cannot remember if I gasped and choked and sank and had to be
lifted out of the water with strong arms or if I somehow
made it to the shore, but I know that now I love the
water; I love to feel my body moving through it and I
love to feel the surf of a roaring ocean breaking over my
head and I like the feeling of swimming out until I am
enervated and then drifting back, exhausted but strong
enough, strong enough. In the summers when I was
young I swam in a pond that was long and wide and
deep, and between the pond and the old stone house
was an agéd apple orchard, the trees lined on the rises
of the rolling lawn. There was a garden beyond the
trees, not a small domestic garden with a few straggly
offerings of flowers, but a garden, bordered on one side
by a row of weeping willows whose lacy branches undu-
lated slowly in the wind, rustling, where thousands of
narcissus and daffodils bloomed in the early spring, followed by bright patches of tulips and then by large
stands of irises, ranging in color from the lightest
salmon pink to black, and then followed by extravagant
bursts of peonies. In the late spring the apple trees
seemed to come into blossom all at once and I remember walking under them and looking up through
the pink mist into a clear blue sky and I remember the
petals floating on the water of the pond and browning
and rotting in the grass beneath the trees. Later, in the
summer, the trees bristled with tiny hard apples, and
the strings of frogs' eggs that had been laid earlier had

hatched into swarms of tadpoles that blackened the water's edge and moved in eddies although there was no current. Those summer days, and later, when the sun burned the leaves on the apple trees to a green-red-brown and the apples swelled and darkened, I swam and played, but still I was a child.

In the winters, when I was young, when I could not be in the water, my father taught me how to play the piano and I can remember that clearly. My father played—he had studied piano in college but then had gone to Wall Street, as I did, and sometimes, when he played for guests, which he could occasionally be coaxed to do although he said he did not enjoy it ("I play for myself," he would say, "I am not a performer."), the guests would ask him why he had given up a career in music for one on Wall Street and he would say, as some gangster once said when asked why he robbed banks, "It's where the money is," and shrug his shoulders. When I was very small, before I studied piano, I loved to listen to him play, sometimes rocking in my little rocking chair with a book in my lap—I can remember one book that had vivid, stylized illustrations of lions, tigers, and elephants peering through tall grasses, but I cannot remember what the book was about—and sometimes sitting beside him and sometimes, and this was the most fun, lying on my back under the piano. When I lay under the piano he would sometimes switch abruptly from a piece that was soft and lyrical to one that was loud, harsh, and percussive, and I would scream and laugh and beat my heels against the carpet. I can even remember some of the things he played when I was so young. The first thing I remember him playing was the music of Bach, and although then I did not know the names of the pieces, now I know that he often played preludes and fugues from *The Well-Tempered Clavier* and he often played the *Goldberg Variations,* which now I often listen to and play myself, although I no longer have the strength to play through all of them without resting, and each time I hear that opening theme, so austere yet so lush, I am returned to my childhood.

Later, but still when I was young, I began to recognize the Chopin waltzes, particularly the one in C-sharp minor with its slow, burlesquey opening theme with the little scherzo-like skip in it, followed by the quick and light descending figure in the outside of the right hand that falls away to the thumb, and I also remember his two "war-horses," as he called them, which were Schumann's *Symphonic Etudes* and Rachmaninoff's *Piano Sonata No. 2.* When I heard him start the slow, quiet theme of the *Symphonic Etudes* I would run in from wherever I was in the house and listen, impatient with the slow variations (I was young then, as I have said; now I enjoy the slow variations and wish they would go on forever and sometimes I play just one of them again and again) and excited by the fast ones, but my favorite was the last variation, which is big and loud, and when it started I would jump up and roar out in my little boy's voice, "bum bum bum bum Bum **BUM** Bum bum. . . ," and stamp my foot at the big chord that is the climax of the first phrase. But most of all I loved the Rachmaninoff sonata and when he played it I would march around the room stamping my feet and singing loudly.

I grew older, and as I aged my body became taut and hard, agile and strong. I learned to play the piano myself, starting with the little pieces all children play but within two or three years progressing to easy Bach and Chopin. I can remember that when I started my first Chopin—it was an easy prelude, I think, or perhaps a mazurka—I was so happy that I was playing *Chopin* that I played the piece again and again, and I remember my mother coming to the door of the living room and saying that it sounded like a needle was stuck on a record. I still loved the water, but now, in the summers, I swam in the sea, so cold it made me ache, and because I was still young I took all of it at once, running along the top of a rock on the Maine shore and diving into the water, and the shock of the cold made me gasp. I did not paddle and play but swam hard until I could stand the cold no longer and then ran out and climbed to the top of my rock and lay naked in the sun, watching my penis resume its normal size after it had retreated from the cold of the water. Sometimes then I would masturbate, and when I did I usually thought about boys, not girls, and I thought about touching someone who was thin and hard and strong, as I was, and then later I would again dive into the frigid water and wash the stickiness from the thin line of light hair that was forming down the center of my stomach.

One year instead of going to the sea I went to the mountains and I swam in a lake that was cold, although not as cold as the sea, and so clean that the bottom was faintly visible even far from shore, the light, scattered by the waves on the surface and filtered through the water, making it seem to move. I was fifteen then, and every day I swam and my body became harder and stronger and my hair faded to light blond, and then in the middle of the summer a family came to the cottage next to ours which had not been opened for several years. I was swimming toward our dock, I remember, when a boy came out on the dock that belonged to the empty cottage and looked out at the lake. He had dark hair and a dark tan and he wore white pants and white shoes and he stood on the dock with his hands in his pockets, and even though I was cold from the water I got an erection. I did not see him for another day but I watched the activity in the house, the opening of windows and the repeated trips out to the car and the loud sounds of banging. The following day a man strung a rope between two old pines that had no branches below ten feet or so, and the boy came out with armloads of blankets and hung them over the rope. I watched through the screen while I lay on my stomach on my bed—a single bed that was more like a cot—with my chin on the windowsill. After the boy hung the blankets

I watched for more than an hour and he did not come back out so I changed into trunks, masturbating first so my erection would recede, and went down to the lake. I ran out on the dock and dove into the water without stopping and swam underwater as long and as far as I could and when I came up the boy was running down his dock and as I watched he dove in and swam under water and came up only a few feet from me. I remember that he shook his head and said, "It's cold!" and I told him that it wasn't as cold as the ocean, but the only ocean he had swum in was in the south and he did not know. I can still remember that one day so clearly, like yesterday, as the saying goes; we swam until we were chilled and our hands were wrinkled from the water and we climbed out on my dock and shared my towel because he had not brought one with him. We looked at each other carefully, I remember; I was, as I have said, strong and lithe, as I always was until I became ill, and he was shorter than I was, with stocky, muscular legs and muscular buttocks. I did better than he did in the penis department, although I did not know it then and it never mattered to either of us.

After that first day we were almost never apart, and we always knew, from that first day, that there was a sexual dimension to our friendship, which did not make us uncomfortable as much as anxious to know what would happen. We talked about girls a lot, I remember, but we talked about other things too, like what we thought about when we masturbated—he often thought about me and I about him, and we said, "You know, we've got to *do it* sometime," and we knew we would, but we did not know when and it did not bother us too much that we did not. We used our energy, which I now know was partially sexual, in other ways: we swam hard, we cleared the woods around our cottages with axes and saws, we ran miles together, and we often sat out on either my dock or his until late at night watching the lights around the lake shimmering across the water and listening to the waves lap at the smooth stones at its edge, and sometimes we touched casually. Our families left us on our own (my mother was there most of the time and my father came for long weekends), each relieved that their son had found a friend, and frequently they would both be away, leaving us to cook for ourselves, and when they did our dinner was always the same: hot dogs and potato salad. He made the salad. Surprisingly, when we actually decided to make love— we called it "doing it," as I have said—we were very nervous, although we had discussed it often. Also surprising, it was not at night, the first time, although we always slept in either my room or his when our parents were away, but it was in the morning after we had spent the night together, in my room, in separate beds, and we decided to go for a swim before breakfast. The air was cold and steam rose from the water and we screamed boys' screams as we ran out on the dock and dove into the water, and we swam until we were cold and then climbed out and ran back to my cottage. We were shivering and we turned on the shower and both got in with our trunks on and, although we were careful not to touch each other more than was made necessary by the logistics of getting under the water and then moving aside so that the other could enjoy the hot water's full force, we could see that we both had erections. It did not happen as you might think, with an occasional accidental touch prolonged until we were touching each other's penises and then getting out and moving to the bed; instead, one of us, I think it was I although I do not really remember, said abruptly, "So, let's do it," or something similar, and we both took off our trunks and laughed at our erections popping up and we stood under the water for a few more minutes pulling each other's penises before we got out and went to my room. Neither of us had any experience and we both gagged on each other and we both, as I think I said (my memory fails me sometimes these days), screwed the other, and I remember that it hurt me a lot because although my penis was longer, his was fatter, and at first he could not get it in so he pushed harder and harder until it went in all at once and I yelled.

We passed the summer swimming and playing in the water and racing boats across the lake. We fished too; from the docks we caught perch with rough scales and sharp fins and sometimes, in the early morning when the light was gray and the lake was still and pearly vapor rose from its surface, we trolled for trout, moving as slowly as the motor would go without dying and stringing our lines out far behind, well weighted so they would sink into the cooler water below, where the big ones were. Some mornings we caught nothing and finally, when the morning sun began to make us uncomfortable in our sweaters, we turned back, disappointed and quiet, but when even one of us made a catch, when it was time to stop we would roar back toward the shore and, when in sight of our cottages, whoop and shout. When we docked we cleaned our catch on a flat stone by the water, using his hunting knife, and then ran to either his place or mine, usually his, and cooked our fish. It made our parents smile to see us, to see us being boys doing the things that boys do, but we still did other things too; we made love and explored each other's bodies and mouths and we were happy. We both left in late August, I remember, and I cried, secretly, and although we had promised to keep in touch, after a few months we wrote less frequently and then not at all and the next summer another part of my family used the place at the lake and I returned to Maine. We never saw each other again, but even now, more than ten years later, I still remember that summer.

When I think about it now it seems that the next four years went quickly and easily, although I remember when I was living through them they did not seem so tranquil. In the summers I swam in the ocean in Maine and I also began to learn the sport I loved so much, rock-climbing. I can remember so clearly that first climb, with an instructor, on the cliffs along the Maine shore. I was terrified. We started at the top of the cliffs and as I looked over the edge and felt the cool updraft from the sea and saw the brightly colored buoys from the lobster pots bobbing and twisting in the waves just a few yards from the narrow band of rocks at the bottom of the cliffs I felt as though I was slowly acting a part in a dream that I could not control, and when my instructor—a beautiful man who was, I thought then and now know, straight—told me to stand on the edge of the cliff with my back toward it and then put his hand on the upper part of my arm to guide me into place I thought I would be sick, and when, upon his instruction, I leaned back on the ropes until my back was out over the cliff and I could hear the sea breaking against the rocks below I was, I thought, prepared to die. I made it down, of course, walking slowly backward down the face of the cliff until I reached the bottom, and when I stood on the rocks that were wet with the spray from the waves I was so relieved my eyes teared, and getting down was much easier than climbing back up. I was fit and limber, but on the face of that cliff I felt as weak and uncoordinated as a small child. My instructor climbed up first, showing me where to put my hands and feet and placing chocks and little devices called Friends into cracks in the rock for protection. When he was on the top he roped himself to anchors behind him and then leaned over the cliff to watch me. He must have been amused. I tried to make the climb mainly by pulling myself up with my arms—I had thought I was strong—forgetting, in my fear, everything he had told me about using my feet, and I fell off again and again, and although I was always caught and held by the ropes and I never fell more than a foot or two I was still paralyzed by fear every time I fell. When my head finally reached over the top, instead of pushing myself up until I could reach the top with my foot I scrambled up using my hands and elbows and knees, scaping them badly (it took several weeks for the abrasions to heal completely). I have made many climbs since that day, and I wish that I could just once more feel the warmth of the sun on the backs of my legs as I stretch them to their limits on the side of a cliff and once more feel the thrill and then the calm that comes at the end of a difficult climb when you sit on the top of a cliff or the summit of a mountain and look out over the world, but I know that I will not, and still I remember that first climb so clearly.

In the winters, during those years, I continued to work at the piano, and during one of the winters, when I was in high school and still living at home, I finally learned the *Symphonic Etudes* that I had always loved. I practiced them when my father was at work, or away, as he often was—he spent almost as much time at the London office of his company as he did at the office in New York; it was my mother's and my secret. I remember when I first played them for him. He had just come back from a trip somewhere—to British Columbia, I think—and he was sitting in a chair in the living room reading his mail with a drink on the table beside him, and I sat at the piano and played a little Chopin mazurka that was in the same key and then immediately began the *Etudes*. I could not see him because the chair was behind me, but I heard him put the mail on the floor beside himself and get up and at first I played carefully and deliberately but then I was swept away by the music—all Romantic piano music should be played by passionate, impetuous teenagers—and I took risks and missed notes but it went well and when I came to the last variation, the one that I had loved as a small child, my father came to the front of the piano and watched me and then sang out with the theme, as I had done, "bum bum bum bum Bum **BUM** Bum bum. . . ," and slapped his hand against the top of the piano at the big chord. When I was finished, I remember, he told me that I played it better than he did and although I disagreed, I knew that it was true.

I still swam in the winters, too, in pools, and I grew into a solid, strong young man, and through my first two years of college I secretly sought and found other young men, but I was not satisfied. I spent the summer when I was twenty in the mountains, not at the old place on the lake, which had been sold, but at a cabin in the woods in the Adirondacks that was more than five miles from the nearest lake and even farther from any river. The cabin belonged to a distant relative—the father of an aunt by marriage, I think—who allowed me to use it for the summer if I would, as he said, fix it up a little. The place had not been cared for in years; the roof leaked, hinges were broken or rusty, windows were cracked, a step was missing, the floor was sagging, and a thick growth of bushes and seedlings had come up around it. I was lonely at the beginning of that summer. During the days I worked hard on the property, cleaning, repairing and painting the cabin, clearing the woods, and improving the bumpy, overgrown tire tracks that had been worn into the ground and formed the only access to the public road, which was almost a quarter of a mile away and, even then, only a narrow gravel road. That road wove up and down hills for three miles until it reached a macadam road, and in the afternoons I would go for a hard run to the macadam road and back, usually shirtless, and I remember that feeling, tiring but exhilarating, of running the hills, and I remember that when a car passed I would be covered with dust, which I could feel in my throat and taste in my mouth and which stuck to my sweat, and how I wish I could feel that feeling of running hard and sweating and being covered with dust in the hot sun on an isolated mountain road just once again in my life.

The cabin, that summer, had electricity that was supplied by a gasoline-powered generator, but often, instead of running the generator to pump water for a shower, after my run I would pull off my shoes and get into my little car and drive to the public beach at the lake. Sometimes after I swam I would dress and go to a small church, overlooking the lake and surrounded by pines, where I had received permission to practice. The piano I used there was ancient and untunable but I was happy to have access to it. Sometimes, however, after I swam I sat on my towel alone on the beach, waiting for someone to speak to me and sad and disappointed when they did not. I knew then that I was gay and thought that I was attractive and I hungered for some of the other young men I saw at the lake, if only as friends; however, they were all straight and interested only in impressing girls, and each other.

The walk to the beach passed the town's tennis courts and often on my way back to my car I stopped and hung on to the chain fence with my fingers and watched the people taking tennis lessons, my towel hanging around my neck. Most of the students were either women or boys, the wives, daughters, and young sons of the rich, and I found them uninteresting, but the instructor was to me a Golden God, with a great mane of blond hair and solid, powerful legs that were well-tanned and covered with more blond hair. He always wore white shorts and a sleeveless T-shirt, and I often stood and watched him play, watching the muscles in his legs tensing and contracting as he moved and admiring his shoulders shining with sweat, until I could feel the swelling of an erection, and then I wrapped my towel around my waist and walked slowly to my car, and at home I masturbated. I remember so well the day we finally met; I can almost reach out and touch him still. It was a hot, intermittently rainy day, and as I ran my usual route the heat and the high humidity made the sweat run into my eyes and down my back and stomach, and when I got back to the cabin I was completely wet, both from my sweat and from the misty rain that had started as I ran the last mile or two. I did not really want to swim, I remember, but I was feeling alone and sad, and I wanted to be around people, so I spread a towel across the seat of my car and drove to the lake. There was no one in the water and the lifeguards were playing backgammon under a shelter, but when I waded in they all ran out and assumed their posts. I thought it was silly, I remember, because they were all high school students and I was a stronger and better swimmer than any of them. I swam hard, as I did when I was depressed, and when I got out of the water I walked slowly back to the car to get my towel. The tennis courts were wet and deserted, but I looked to see if the pro was there. He was not; however, when I got to the street he was sitting on the hood of my car drinking a beer. I said hello, shyly, and when he asked if it was my car and I said yes he apologized and jumped down. He offered me a beer from a small cooler and I took it, although I wasn't much of a drinker and didn't like beer at all, and when I finished it he asked me if I was interested in smoking some good hashish, "hash," he called it. I had never used drugs before but I said yes and we went to his apartment, which faced the lake the beach was on. I got so high I couldn't walk, and he fucked me hard.

I was sad the next day, I remember, because it had not been what I had expected. He had no affection for me and I had a crush on him. I worked hard that day with an ax, attacking the seedlings that had grown into small trees around the cabin until my shoulders ached, and then I ran harder and farther than usual, and when I went to the lake I swam until I was exhausted. He waved to me when he saw me pass on the way back to the car but he did not come to the fence to speak and I was hurt, and I was angry. That summer was, in retrospect, one of the best of my life and one of the worst. I grew even stronger and I knew that I looked good, and I loved being in the woods, falling asleep and waking again to the sounds of nature and the sweet scent of the larches, those most exquisite conifers with their soft light-green needles that drop in the winter, that surrounded the cabin. I hated being alone, though, and I could think of no one but the tennis pro—how foolish that seems now but how real it was then. We had sex occasionally; he used me if there wasn't anyone around he wanted more. He slept with women too, and I think he treated them the same way, but at that time I did not care how he treated me as long as he noticed me and I did not care how selfish he was sexually; I could always masturbate later.

That fall, back at school, I searched the gay bars and the streets and the campus for my Ideal; I guess now I'd call it Blond and Butch and laugh a little, although then I was very serious and looked only for a replacement for my Golden God. During the day I was almost myself, although I did often find myself staring at some handsome man without realizing what I was doing and when I became conscious of it my face became warm and a pink flush rose from my chest to my neck. I went to my classes and studied and swam and ran and practiced the piano, but then as it became darker I began to become more excited and it became more and more difficult to concentrate on my studies until finally, when it was night but still early, almost never later than ten o'clock, I began my search. I went to the park, moving slowly from one shadow to another, and watched the men, and when I saw one I liked I would approach him quickly and put my hand on his crotch, and then, if my hand was not pushed away, and it almost never was, I would kneel in front of the man and take all of him and if he did not put his hands on the back of my head I would place them there myself. Sometimes the man would turn my face to a wall or a tree and fuck me, and sometimes he left me still kneeling in front of him until he was finished, but it did not matter. Sometimes, however, there was no one in the park, or at least no one I liked, although I do admit that almost any man was fine with me, and when there was no one I would turn to the bars.

I did not like bars because I did not like to drink, both because I did not have much love for alcohol and because I thought it was a waste of both time and money, so I went to bars where the cruising was open and explicit and I went to bars that had back rooms. I liked the bars with back rooms; I liked to stand against the bar massaging my crotch until I got an erection and until I caught someone's eye, both of which usually happened soon, and then have him follow me into the darkness, where I would give myself to him for ten minutes, or however long it took. I seldom went home with men—I could not bring them back to my dorm—and when I did I would resist all attempts of my partner of the moment to make casual conversation; I wanted only sex. When we were finished I would never spend the night, although I was often asked, and sometimes when I left, if it was early enough, I went back to the bars for more. That was how I met Ted. He was the second of the night, preceded by a sultry Puerto Rican whose name I cannot remember but whose dick I can.

Ted was, I thought, the person I had been looking for. He was blond and hot—he was, as I used to say, *physical*—and he took me to his apartment. It was in a horrible walk-up building in Hell's Kitchen; reeking winos and drug addicts shivered on the stoops and there were prostitutes on the corner who said hello to Ted and called him honey. As we neared his building I remember that a woman grabbed his arm and asked him for $1.50 for, as she said, the subway to Staten Island (there is no subway to Staten Island) and Ted laughed and gave her a subway token and, as the woman walked away cursing, Ted told me that the liquor store on the corner had bottles of wine for $1.50, including tax, and I can remember that when we came to his building I looked up at it and said, "Maybe this isn't such a good idea," and he laughed and took my arm and led me inside and I did not resist. It would be romantic, I guess, to be able to say that we made love on a mattress thrown on the floor in the middle of a dirty, bare apartment, but it was not true. Like him, his apartment was beautiful, with exposed brick walls and a fireplace and polished hardwood floors—I learned later that he had done all of the work himself—and we made love on a shiny brass bed. We made love for a long time, I remember, and when we finished I sat up and began looking around for my underwear and Ted asked me where I was going, and when I said I was leaving he pulled me down and we made love again. I can still remember the next morning so clearly; it was November and the leaves were gone from the trees and it was cold and gray and damp. I was in a hurry to get out, I remember, and as I dressed, he dressed, and when I put on my coat he put on his, and when I asked him where he was going he said he was walking me home. It makes me smile to remember it, because we really did walk the seventy-five blocks back to my dorm, laughing and talking and touching sometimes, and I was happy.

Chapter 2

It makes me smile to remember Ted—I used to call him my Teddy Bear, although he looked nothing like a bear at all. He was five years older than I, and taller and stronger (he had been working out at a gym since he was nineteen), and he always looked so good, not at the end, of course, but when we met and during the first years we were together he was so hand-

some, not rugged but with smooth, tight, rounded muscles. Sometimes he looked almost delicate, although
physically and sexually he was not delicate at all—it
was, I guess, his face, which was thin but with soft
lines (no high, sharp cheekbones) and a dimple in each
cheek, that made him look delicate—and I do miss
him so much, and how I wish that I could see him just
once again as he was that November we met or as he
was those first two summers we were together on Fire
Island, when his skin turned golden brown and his hair
dazzled in the sun, not to tell him about myself but just
to hold his hand or to embrace him, or even just to
share a bottle of St. Pauli Girl, the beer he always
drank (he told me he remembered being on the Island
an earlier summer when planes flew low over the beach
trailing streamers advertising it, and that summer was
the summer I had spent in the mountains and first had
sex with a boy). I remember those first few weeks we
spent together so well. That November it seemed never
to stop raining, sometimes just a little drizzle that Ted
would call spit—"it's spitting out," he'd say—and
sometimes wind-driven torrents that came off the Hud-
son and the harbor and raged against the city, when
water ran swift and deep in the gutters and collected in
pools at intersections where the drains were clogged
and ran in sheets down the window by Ted's bed, and I
cannot think of Ted without remembering the sight and
smell of bare, wet trees in the park dripping under a
gray sky and without remembering the reflection of

streetlights and headlights on the wet sidewalks and pavement. We often walked in the rain sharing an umbrella with our arms around each òther's waists, and we were not self-conscious doing it, either from a desire to make an impression on those who saw us or from a feeling that we were doing something wrong. No, we were in love, as I understand what that means—this is sentimental, I know, but even now sometimes when I remember those times tears come to my eyes and I do not apologize—and of course I cannot explain it but I know how I felt, excited when I was going to see him and so close to him when we were together that it seemed like we were one and missing him when we were apart, and I know how much I miss him still.

That first morning after we met, when Ted walked with me back to my dorm, I remember that when we got there Ted said, "Tonight?" I had been hoping that he would ask to see me again and I agreed instantly and he laughed and gave me a big hug and a kiss and told me that I was "easy," and I remember wondering in that instant, for the first time, if my sexual practices— quick, uncomplicated sex with as many people as possible in as short a time as possible—might not be something to be ashamed of (now I am not ashamed) and then the thought dissolved and I laughed and put my hand on his crotch, not caring whether I was seen, and I said, "You bet." I can remember some of that day after he left and before I saw him again. My first class of the morning was Latin—I have always loved the logic, structure, and clarity of that language, and it still satisfies me to read a few pages of Apuleius or Petronius or Ovid and when I do I feel as though I am in a different world, in a different time, and when I read medieval Latin I feel drenched in the mysteries of the Dark Ages—and I could not concentrate and the professor (I cannot remember his name) remarked to the class, after I had not even heard a question addressed to me, that I must be in love, and when I blushed the professor said, "Oh, he *is* in love," and everyone laughed, and I was very embarrassed. I had not thought of it that way before, but for the rest of the day I tested the phrase and the idea carefully and I decided that I was: In Love. I know that sounds foolish and trite and sentimental and banal and like a horrible cliché, but when you are experiencing this, and every person— man or woman, gay or straight—has, I hope, experienced it at least once, it does not seem banal or trite or any of the other disparaging things: It is wonderful. I remember that I practiced the piano that afternoon and I played like a wild man; it was not a time for slow, careful practice, it was a time to just play and enjoy it, and I did. I played some sweet Chopin nocturnes and then played every fast, banging, clattering piece I knew, missing notes and playing too fast and too loud and abusing the damper pedal, and as I played I became aware that people were outside the practice room listening and looking through the little window in the door, and I gave them a good show. I ended with a piece by Liszt—"Vallée d'Oberman"—that starts slowly, with great feeling, and then builds to a tremendous climax of octaves surging up and down the keyboard, and although I have often played the piece since then I have never played it better.

It grew very cold that evening and when I reached Ted's apartment I could see my breath in the air. He had a fire in the fireplace when I came in, I remember, and when he answered the door he had a glass of wine in his hand and when I kissed him he smelled winey, but it did not matter. We spoke very little but were, within a few minutes, naked and clutching each other as tightly as two strong men can and then rolling and holding and kissing and biting and rubbing and making love—I intentionally do not call it fucking because this was different; it was not the best sex I had ever had, but it was the best sex I ever had with someone I loved, and yes I know I only met him the night before, but if you have never felt like that do not criticize me, because my feelings were genuine, and if you have felt like that, you understand what I mean better than I could ever tell you.

After we made love we showered together, I remember, and we almost made love again but we knew that there would be time later and we reluctantly dressed, frequently stopping to touch or kiss, and then we went out for dinner. It was clear, which was unusual that November, and quite cold, and Ted wore a black leather bomber jacket—it hangs in my closet now and I wonder if I will live until it is cold enough to wear it again—and he was so handsome. We could see our breath in the air as we walked, and although it was cold we did not wear gloves and did not put our hands in our pockets but we held each other's hand and swung our arms. We had dinner in an old tavern on Eleventh Avenue that had been there for a very long time (I once knew how long, but I have forgotten) and all the employees knew Ted. When we came in, as we walked past the bar on our way to a table in the back corner of the room Ted said, "Two of the usual," to the bartender, and when we were seated a waitress brought us two martinis, without ice. I had never drunk a martini before and I remember telling Ted that I couldn't drink it, and he told me that it was good for me—he called it Vitamin M. "It'll loosen you up," he said. I hated it, but I drank it, and while I drank one, Ted drank three, and then he ordered a carafe of red wine with our dinner. I can even remember what we ate (he ordered for both of us)—steaks, cottage fries, and green salads, with cheese cake for dessert—and I wonder what it is about the mind that sometimes takes significant events and surrounds them with a little circle of clear memory so that not only the event is remembered clearly (in this case falling in love with Ted) but also many of the inconsequential details of life that accompany the event are remembered clearly as well: the weather, smells, food, a newspaper headline. I can also remember that when we left I was drunker than I had ever been before and I was weaving and stumbling and Ted, who seemed to be completely sober, put his arm around my waist and said that I would feel better if we took a walk, and he took me on a *long* walk.

We walked over to Ninth Avenue and then uptown and then across to Columbus Circle and then back downtown. We stopped to look at a poster outside a gay porno theater (I remember that the main feature was called *Loving Hands*) and Ted said, "Come on, let's go in," and although I protested, eventually I agreed. We sat in the back next to the wall on the left, I remember, and I can also remember how shocked I was at what I was seeing on the screen. I had seen pornography, of course, and I had been very active sexually, but I had never seen or experienced anything other than normal gay sex, by which I mean sex as it is practiced by the majority of gay men. Ted was very excited by the film and he placed my hand in his lap and then moved my fingers to make them unbutton a button and then I unbuttoned the rest without guidance and he put his hand on my neck and pulled me sideways and pushed my head down. I resisted at first, not because I did not enjoy the activity involved—I had done it countless times—or because I objected to the public place—it was probably more private than the backroom bar that I often had sex in and where I met him—but because it did not seem right to be doing it there with someone I loved, and I know now that I *did* love him from that first day and, although later we

27

fought terribly and were cruel and mean to each other,
I know now that I never stopped loving him, and although it was so few years ago it seems like so many.
That night, our Second Night, I ended up kneeling on
the floor of the theater with my face in his crotch, and
although I was uncomfortable then, now I do not regret
it at all.

From that evening we were almost always together at
night. I would sleep at his apartment and then get up
and go to class and sometimes go to my dorm to collect
mail or to get clothes, and in the late afternoons I practiced piano, impatient to see him but knowing that he
did not get home from work until later. (I think I said
that he was a mostly out-of-work actor who supple-
mented his income by working, sometimes during the
day and sometimes in the evening, as a clerk on Wall
Street and that I work on Wall Street too, and although
I no longer go to the office I still do conduct some business by telephone, but I do not remember.) I spend a
lot of time now remembering and thinking about the
process of remembering, and I do not understand why I
can clearly remember events and people from years ago
but I cannot remember things from only a week ago,
like the name of the handsome guy who came to visit
last week because my regular GMHC Buddy was out of
town. The guy was so nice, too. We went out to
lunch—he wanted to pay, but I would not let him because the one thing I do have is money. The young
man—maybe his name is Greg, or Gary—held my

hand on the way back from the restaurant. He left while I was napping, but he wrote me a nice note and left it leaning against the toaster in the kitchen, and the daisies he brought are still in front of me.

Thanksgiving break came three weeks after I met my Teddy Bear and it was the first time we were apart for more than a day. It rained hard the day I left (did I say that my family's home was in Connecticut?), and I remember going back to my dorm from Ted's that Wednesday morning and packing a few things in a duffel bag and being sad because I would be away and because I did not have the courage to take Ted home with me. When I was packed I called him at work to say good-bye, I remember, and he asked me if I wanted to meet him at his apartment during his lunch hour, and of course I agreed. I took a bus down, I remember, but it was raining hard and I was wet when I got to his apartment and he had not arrived. The outside door was locked (he had offered me keys but I had not accepted them) and I pressed myself into the doorway, shielding myself with my umbrella, trying to keep dry, but the wind blew the rain down the street in sheets—it made patterns of moving ribbons of water on the pavement— and by the time Ted arrived I was almost totally wet from my knees to my feet. Ted came in a cab and when it stopped in front of the building he got out and ran up the steps holding a newspaper over his head, and I re- member that when he gave me a kiss his face was wet. He was in a hurry and we barely spoke but we rushed in and he pounded the elevator button in his impatience and as soon as we were upstairs and inside he began to kiss me roughly and I responded the same way, and within a few minutes we were making love so roughly that it was almost violent, and as soon as he finished he dressed quickly and said that he had to get back to work. We kissed good-bye on the steps in front of his building and as we kissed a cab came down the street and he ran out and stopped it and got in, and he was gone. I walked to Grand Central Station in the rain, almost crying, and I can remember that already I missed him.

It was still raining when I got off the train in Connecticut, and I can remember that I was cold and that my mother was not there waiting and I had to stay on the platform, exposed to the wind-driven rain from the sides, until she arrived. My mother is, I have been told by many people, an "incredible woman" (sometimes, even now, I wish she were a little less "incredible"). This makes me remember that the first time I was in the hospital, four months ago, a nurse left the room, when Mother was there, without doing something that Mother thought she should have done, and Mother opened the door and yelled out into the hall in a voice that would have stopped a truck, *"Get back in here!"* But back to the day I was telling about. She drove into the station parking lot at about fifty miles per hour honking the horn and waving, and when I ran to the car she got out in the rain and held the back door open for me to throw my bag inside, and then I ran around to the other side of the front and when I got in she leaned across the seat and gave me a big kiss. I remember that she told me that she had to do a little more shopping, "for just a few more things," I'm sure she said, and we shopped for hours, buying bread, flowers, pastries, cheese, fruit, and assorted groceries in half a dozen stores, and then we went to several more stores looking for a perfect wicker basket to put on the table the next day, and throughout the afternoon I could not stop thinking about Ted. Most gay men I know sometime in their lives decide that they want to tell their parents that they are gay, and I am sure that many gay men, when they have made this decision, feel as I felt that day, apprehensive, even slightly frightened at the possible reaction, feeling my heart beat in my chest and trying to choose the right words and knowing that I had to say something but afraid of hurting my parents' feelings. I remember that finally, when we found the basket Mother wanted and were driving toward home—I can even remember that we were passing a high stone wall on the right—I was filled with such pressing tension that I could no longer be silent and I blurted out, with no introduction, "Mother, I'm gay," and Mother, bless her, turned toward me and said, "I know, dear." I slid down in the seat, way down, and laughed until I almost cried, both with relief and at the way my mother had said, "I know, dear," as if I had been delivering some completely ordinary, trite bit of information, like that the day was

31

Wednesday or that it was raining, and I remember that Mother laughed too and when I was able to speak again I asked her how she knew and she said, and I remember these words clearly too, "Mothers always know these things." I remember that she asked me if I was happy and I told her about Ted, but not about any other part of my gay life, and then I asked her if my father knew and she said that they had never discussed it and that it was my responsibility to tell him if I wanted him to know, not hers, and my tension and apprehension came back again even stronger until I felt ill.

It felt strange carrying my bag to my old room. Although Columbia was only an hour-long train ride away (did I say that I attended Columbia and that I studied music and philosophy? I cannot remember), I had not come home at all that fall, telling my family that I was busy with schoolwork but really spending time in the bars and parks searching for men, and I had declined my father's many invitations to have lunch or dinner with him in the city. That day I was at the same time happy to see my old things—my swimming medals from high school, a three-foot-high stuffed toy penguin that had been a gift, my old desk, my books and music—and sad that Ted was not with me, and somehow I felt that I had passed a barrier that I could never go back through and that I would never again be my parents' son and that their house would never again be my home, and I know now that, although my parents have been loving and supportive and I love them very much, my intuition that day was accurate: My relationship with my parents has never been the same. It is not worse, if anything it is better, but it is completely different. I think that parents of gay sons and daughters cannot help being disappointed that there will probably never be spouses, children, grandchildren, and that therefore their sons' and daughters' lives will be completely different from their own, foreign, but some parents accept this and try to understand these different lives and try to find a place for themselves in them, and that place is a different place than they would have had in the lives of their straight children. That day, I remember, I looked at my books and then at my music, looking for some pieces to read through at the piano, and I took out a volume of Bach's keyboard music. I had not played much of Bach's music—I preferred the great Romantic works of Chopin, Liszt, Brahms (that fall I played the F minor Sonata *very* passionately, but not very well), Schumann, and Rachmaninoff—but the volume I picked up had the *Goldberg Variations* in it, which my father had played for me when I was young (he did not play as much at the time I am telling about, although he was still very good) and I worried about the conversation I knew I was going to have with him, and I took the music to the piano and began to play.

I can never forget that first time I played those beautiful *Variations*. They are very difficult, and I could not play them at the tempo they should be played at and I worked hard, and I was thinking about Ted and about telling Mother I was gay and worrying about telling Dad that I was gay, and now when I play them (I can no longer play the fast, difficult variations but I play the slow variations often) they are always accompanied by a surge of memories of that day and of my Teddy Bear and of the good times and the bad times we had, and behind and filtered through these memories are memories of my childhood and my father, and sometimes when I play the *Variations* I will be thinking about Ted and suddenly will remember some day or some incident from many years earlier, and that memory will be clearer than the memory of Ted or of that Thanksgiving Eve. It seems strange to me that I cannot remember eating dinner that evening, but although I have often thought about that day I cannot remember dinner at all and I cannot remember clearly when my father got home, but I remember the three of us—Mother, Dad, and I—sitting in the living room, later in the evening, talking about school and I can remember that my father asked me, and not to taunt me but just for information, if I had a girl friend.

I can remember the next few minutes very clearly. I said no, of course, and then I got up and went to the piano and Mother went to the kitchen to work on the next day's feast (we were having more than a dozen guests for dinner). I don't remember what I played but I do remember that I was very apprehensive and that I felt ill, and when I stopped playing I turned around on the piano bench and faced my father. I did not blurt out the news this time but told it slowly and with great difficulty. I do not remember my words, but I can remember that for a few minutes my father sat back heavily in his chair and looked not like the successful man he was but like one who is defeated. I knew that he was displeased and I was sad that I had caused his displeasure, for I loved my father and did not want to hurt him. Then, when I was already feeling awful he said to me, and I remember it so clearly that it hurts even now to tell about it, "Are you sure?" and when I said that I was sure, he said, "I am so disappointed," and I started to cry. I remember that more than anything else I wanted to talk to Ted, and I ran out of the room and upstairs and tried to call from the telephone in the guest room, but there was no answer (later, during an argument, I learned that he had been home, but with a trick). I went into my own room then and I, an almost grown man of twenty, lay on my stomach and sobbed. I cried for a long time and then my father knocked on my door and called to me and when I did not answer he came in and he sat on my bed and stroked my hair and apologized and gradually I stopped crying and we talked again, and he told me that my life would be more difficult because I was gay but that he and Mother would always love me and that they would do whatever they could to make my life easier for me, and he told me that they would help me whenever I needed help, and then, I remember, he kissed me on my cheek and said good night and left, closing the door behind him.

Chapter 3

The *big* holidays—Thanksgiving and Christmas—had, over the years, become unchanging rituals for my family. Christmas was always celebrated in Maine and I have many fond memories from my childhood of driving through Connecticut, Massachusetts, and up into Maine with a station wagon filled with wrapped gifts to tantalize me (I was always allowed to open one gift on the way, but one of my parents' choice, not mine), and Thanksgiving was celebrated at our home in Connecticut with a dozen or so relatives in attendance. I remember Thanksgiving and Christmas the year I am telling about so well. On Thanksgiving it was cold and raining heavily and when I got up I stood at the window of my old room watching the rain and then went to the guest room to call Ted. The phone rang for a long time before he answered, and I remember that he sounded very hung over, and although I cannot remember exactly what was said I do remember that after I hung up I went back to my room and wrote him a long letter, and last year when I went through his papers and possessions I found it: the ardent love letter of a twenty-year-old, written on lined yellow paper. I was surprised to find it, because after Ted and I finally separated he said that he had thrown out everything that had belonged to me or that I had written, and I have the letter here still and when I read it I miss him so much.

The house was filled with the spicy, sweet smells of Thanksgiving by the time I came downstairs that morning, smells of cranberries cooking for the warm cranberry sauce seasoned with orange, nutmeg, ginger, and mace, smells of onions and celery sautéing in butter, smells of pies, pumpkin, apple, and mince. Mother and our cleaning lady, who always helped Mother on Thanksgiving morning and then went to her own home and cooked another meal, were working at a counter near the stove, and Dad was making his oyster stuffing, which he always made himself with oysters he shucked as he made it. I can remember when he first offered me one, when I was younger, and I hated it—gray, icky, slimy, disgusting thing that it was—but as I grew older I came to love oysters and by the Thanksgiving I am telling about my father and I had made Thanksgiving breakfast part of our annual ritual. We sat on stools on opposite sides of a counter that ran through the center of the kitchen with a pile of oysters between us and shucked them into bowls, and when we opened a particularly choice one we put a few drops of lemon juice and a drop of Tabasco Sauce on it and ate it and washed it down with V-8 juice and coffee. I remember walking into the kitchen that morning and being uncomfortable, and ashamed too that my father had seen me crying, and wondering if he was going to have more to say about my news, and when he saw me he gestured with his oyster knife to the stool across from him, where he had already set out another knife and a small metal bowl for the oysters and a mug for coffee. There was a plate of lemon wedges in the middle of the counter, and Alice, the cleaning lady, brought me a glass of juice and filled the mug when I sat down, and she gave me a kiss on the cheek and said the usual things about how much I had grown—I had stopped growing several years earlier, I thought—and how handsome I had become (she *always* said that), and after talking with her for a few minutes, telling her about school but *not*

about Ted, she went back to work with Mother and I
started working on the oysters. Dad and I shucked in
silence for a while, occasionally eating one but filling
our bowls steadily, and then I remember, so clearly,
my father saying, "I talked to your mother last night,
and we want you to know that we both love you very
much." Without speaking, I offered my father an
oyster, and he accepted it and smiled.

As I think I have said, our family is large, although I
have no brothers or sisters, and a lot of it lives in the
New York City area, and all of the family in the area
comes to our house for Thanksgiving. My grandparents
arrived first that Thanksgiving day, shortly after noon
although dinner was not scheduled until four—Grandfather, a feisty, independent, often disagreeable man
and Grandmother, a quiet, sweet woman, who was seventy-five that Thanksgiving, with a soft voice, a will of
iron, and the stubbornness of a recalcitrant mule.
Grandfather drove (a terror of the highways!) and on the
way to our house he and Grandmother argued about
whether or not he had taken the most direct route, and
of course they continued their argument in the kitchen
after they arrived. As we always did on Thanksgiving,
we served Grandfather some oysters (I had bought
cocktail sauce for him the day before, because when
Grandfather ate an oyster he started by eating a little of
the sauce with a spoon, then dredged the oyster in it
thoroughly, and then followed it with more sauce from a
spoon) and we made Grandmother a whiskey sour, a

very weak whiskey sour since she had a tendency when she had had a little too much to drink to drop the china and then get weepy, and after a while we got them to stop arguing and settled them into the living room and then, as always, Grandmother asked me to play the piano for them. I loved to play, and I certainly did not mind playing for my grandparents; however, it was always a difficult experience when they were together. Grandmother always asked me to play the same piece, Schumann's *Kinderscenen,* and whenever I played it for her, when I came to the "Träumerei" she would say, "That's *so* beautiful," and ask me to repeat it at least once, and sometimes more than once, and then Grandfather would always say, "That's too dreary! How about some Gershwin?" and then the two of them would quarrel while I finished the *Kinderscenen,* and then, when I played the solo piano version of Gershwin's *Rhapsody in Blue,* which my grandfather loved, my grandmother would say every minute or two, "That's too loud!" and my grandfather would tell her to leave the room if she didn't like it, and they would quarrel through the Gershwin. That afternoon I played the *Kinderscenen,* and my grandparents quarreled, and I played the *Rhapsody in Blue,* and they quarreled, and when I got up from the piano they both begged me to play more.

By three that afternoon everyone was there: *The Family,* as Grandfather called them; *The Tribe,* as I called them. In addition to my grandparents there were three aunts, two uncles, and assorted cousins ranging in age from eight or so to my age. One of the male cousins, who was two years younger than I and whom I had not seen for a year, was in his first year of college and he was very handsome, which surprised me. He was one of these people who seem to mature suddenly. A year earlier he had been an awkward adolescent with pimples and unkempt hair, and that year he was taller and more self-assured, and, as I said, very handsome; he carried himself with an easy grace and had a beautiful smile. When we were younger he had spent a couple of weeks one summer in Maine with me and my family, and I remember that I caught him masturbating in the bathroom; he had a very large penis for a boy, and I was shocked. He was very embarrassed when I caught him, I remember, and although I told him that I did it all the time and suggested that we do it together he refused even to talk about it. I had seen him at least once every year since then and I always remembered that day in Maine, and I was sure that he did too. And there he was, grown up all at once.

Every Thanksgiving the Tribe first gathered in the living room, where a fire was kept burning in the fireplace from early morning until the last guest had left, for grilled shrimp and Champagne and, as I had for the previous several Thanksgivings, I played the waiter, refilling glasses and getting fresh bottles from the kitchen and passing shrimp. That year my cousin helped and as we poured Champagne we each refilled the other's glass liberally and frequently and smiled at each other when we did. Even the children were allowed to have a touch of Champagne in their ginger ale and were served in the same Baccarat champagne flutes the adults were, and my cousin—his name was Daniel, and I always called him Daniel, not Dan, and I still do—and I put a little too much Champagne in the children's glasses, which they loved, and I remember that they begged for more. Once, on my way to the kitchen to get another bottle, I went through the dining room and changed the place cards, which were stuck in little paper turkeys, of course, so that Daniel would be sitting next to me. While I was doing this my mother caught me, and she looked at the card I had put next to mine and then shook her finger at me in mock censure, but she said nothing.

I have always called Thanksgiving dinner at our house The Thanksgiving Day Massacre, and that Thanksgiving was typical. Everyone, even I, drank too much good zinfandel, and there were always several loud conversations going on around and across the table at the same time, and we ate turkey with oyster stuffing, and with apple stuffing that Grandmother brought for those who didn't like oysters, and braised chestnuts with brussels sprouts, and turnips and squash and green beans and parsnips, and mashed potatoes, of course, and probably a dozen different relishes and sauces and varieties of pickles, and through it all both my cousin and I answered questions about college. Dessert was, as always, all the usual pies (my favorite is mince pie with brandy), plus ice cream with assorted sundae toppings, *plus* a mountain of petit fours purchased from a local French bakery, *plus*, in the years that my birthday fell on Thanksgiving, a cake with candles. As my father always said, no one ever went hungry on Thanksgiving in our house. I had had a lot of Champagne before dinner and several glasses of wine with dinner and I was, as I am sure you can understand, reasonably inebriated by the end of the meal, and I remember that when we all got up from the table my parents and grandparents and the aunts and uncles all took their coffee to the living room and sat around the fire, and most of the cousins disappeared into the game room to play Ping-Pong or pinball and listen to records, and I went to the kitchen for a bottle of Champagne and glasses and took Daniel up to my room.

Although then I didn't like getting drunk, or even drinking, and these days I cannot drink at all, I must admit that alcohol has often given me the courage to do or say things that I would not do or say otherwise, and it certainly did that afternoon. There was only one chair in my room, at my desk, so we both lay on my bed leaning against the pillows and listened to music and drank Champagne and I remember that I asked my cousin if he remembered the time I had caught him masturbating, and before he could answer I added, "You had the biggest dick I'd ever seen up to then," and then, still before he could answer, I asked him if he still had it. Now, I don't know if I had thought that he lost it or if it had stopped growing, or what, but I remember that I put my hand between his legs to find out. Daniel was really shocked, and he pushed my hand away roughly and moved away and said, "What are you doing! Are you queer or something!" and I remember that our eyes met and instantly he knew that I was. "Christ!" he said, and he got up and left angrily and went downstairs. As I think about that incident I think that I should have been sad or upset, but I was not. When Daniel left I laughed so hard I couldn't stop, and then I got the hiccups. I still see Daniel now—he came to visit just last week—and we have become close friends, and although he really is straight I tell him that I have forgiven him for it, and I still tease him about the size of his penis, telling him that if he ever decides he's gay and word gets around he'll be the most popular young man in New York. He takes all this with good humor though, and the last time I was in the hospital he brought me an enormous chocolate penis; it was about a foot long and so big I could barely get both hands around it, and I had great fun cutting it up and sharing it with my friends and the nurses, and my mother even brought a piece of it to another patient with AIDS whom I was not allowed to visit because he had some particularly contagious disease and the doctors did not want us communicating bacteria to each other.

But I was telling about the holidays. The wind came up hard that Thanksgiving night and the house shook and I heard it dimly through a filter of sleep, and then a branch struck my window and I awakened with a start, and I remember lying there in the dark listening to the sounds of the house and of the trees blowing in the wind and I thought about Daniel and I wanted to call Ted but I did not because I saw from my watch that it was after three in the morning, and I remember that for the first time I thought about what it really meant and would mean to me and to my life to be gay. Some gay men, I think, never really accept that fact that they are gay, and others accept it and embrace it and defiantly throw it in the teeth of the heterosexual world, and yet others are open about it and comfortable with it but calm too, although I think that they could not be so open and comfortable without the advance work done by those who are more blatant—liberationist, as it is sometimes called. I began to think about all of these things that night and somehow my thoughts were carried along by the sounds of the wind and the house and the trees, and occasionally the snap of a branch arrested my thoughts abruptly, but then they ran on. I thought about my father telling me that my life would be more difficult because I was gay and I realized that it was true and I did not see why that should be and I began to be a little angry and I began, too, to wonder about all of the men and women who were gay and whose families were not understanding and I thought about my father's offer of support whenever I needed it, and at some point in all of this I got out of bed and stood at the window.

Just as sometimes we remember certain events so clearly that we almost relive them every time we think about them, so too do we sometimes remember with sharp clarity scenes of extraordinary or unexpected beauty: I remember standing on the shore in Maine when I was seven or eight watching waves break against a cliff under a sky of dark, roiling clouds while in the distance a rainbow shimmered over the turbulent sea; I remember a tropical sunset I saw from beneath a tulip tree that was in heavy, full bloom when I was twelve, when the sun, as it reached the horizon, radiated blazing bands of orange throughout the sky and birds called quietly in the tree over my head; I remember, when I was fifteen, after sleeping in a sleeping bag in a lean-to high in the Adirondacks, awakening to watch the sun appear over the top of Whiteface Mountain and shine across the surface of a small lake, filling the dark, green valley with morning light; and I remember that Thanksgiving night so clearly it could have been last night. Behind our house, but still on our property, was a hill, wooded at its base but with an open meadow on its crest. The rain had stopped and the wind had broken up the heavy layer of clouds and I looked out at the hill in the moonlight and watched small clouds passing quickly over it through an otherwise clear sky. I could see the trees at the base of the hill, their branches stark against the sky and the curve of the hill and their trunks blurred into shadows, and I stood, naked, watching and thinking and sometimes looking at my own body—its shape and definition was softened by the moonlight—and it seemed as though I stood there for hours, although it probably wasn't long at all, and then I got dressed and quietly went downstairs and through the kitchen and out into the night.

As I walked through the trees at the bottom of the hill I looked up, and the picture of the moon and the rushing clouds across its face seen through the branches of the trees will always be with me. I climbed the hill slowly, looking up at the sky and finding the path with my feet, and when I reached the top I turned and looked back. I could see our house and the steeple of a church in the town beyond. The steeple was barely visible in daylight when there were leaves on the trees, but in the moonlight when the trees were bare its sharp geometric shape made it stand out, and beyond the steeple I could see Long Island Sound, dark and indistinct in the frail moonlight, and as I stood there sometimes a cloud would come between the moon and the earth and I could see a faint shadow pass across the land until it disappeared into the darkness of the Sound. It was cold, I remember, and I stood there until I shook and my teeth chattered and then I walked back and when I came into the kitchen my father was sitting there in a bathrobe in the dark—the only light coming from outside—with a snifter of Cognac in his hand. "It's a beautiful night," I remember he said, and I told him about the moon and the bare trees and the clouds and the steeple and the Sound, and he poured some Cognac for me, which I accepted, and we talked about the family and he told me that Mother had told him I had a "special young man," and I told him about Ted and he asked me to bring him to lunch in the city, and then we talked about school, and I remember that when we went back to bed it was after five.

The next day was one of those rare, startlingly clear November days when the air was cold and the sky the color of a robin's egg and when I got out of bed, which was late, I know, but I do not remember exactly when, I stood naked at my window looking out at the hill, sharp against the blue sky in the bright light, and I opened the window wide and, ignoring the cold, inhaled the heavy, fresh, cold smell of the earth drying in the November sun after a hard rain, and then I put on a pair of shorts and went to call Ted. My dormitory was closed until that Sunday and I wanted to see him so much and I wanted to ask him if I could stay with him until Sunday—I had not told him that my birthday was that Saturday—and I remember that I let the phone ring a long time, perhaps for thirty rings, before I gave up. He had told me that he had the entire weekend off, but nevertheless I called the place where he worked, which I had never done before so it took some time to get the precise phone number, and the person who answered told me that Ted was away for the weekend. I felt as though I had been hit in the stomach.

I went back to my room, I remember, and sat on my bed for a while without thinking, and then dressed in gray sweats and went for a long run (there was no one in the house, but I remember that Mother had left out a plate of croissants along with careful instructions on how to heat them). I ran first to the top of the hill and looked toward the Sound, which was clearly visible and dark blue under the lighter blue of the sky, and beyond it Long Island appeared as a dark band separating the Sound from the sky. There were a few white sails on the water and I remembered earlier years when I would sail as late in the fall as possible, finally allowing the boat to be pulled out sometime in December, and now as I think about sailing I remember a wonderful sail Ted and I had the following summer when I managed to pry him away from The Pines on Fire Island and take him to Maine for a week. My family no longer kept a boat in Maine then, but I rented a victory sloop from friends who lived there year around. Victory sloops were the workboats of the nineteenth century, sturdy and easy to sail, and a few boat builders in Maine still make them, although now they are used for pleasure and for tourists. Ted did not like the water as I did—he loved the beach but he probably didn't go into the water more than four or five times all summer—and he had never sailed. The first day we had the boat was quite windy, but the bay was fairly calm and I was eager to be out on the water. I remember Ted protesting that two of us could not possibly sail such a large boat by ourselves (it was only thirty-five feet), but I laughed and told him that I could sail it myself if I had to. I used the engine to pull away from the dock but then I killed it, and I remember Ted saying "What happened!" and then saying that he wished he'd brought a thermos of martinis. I sailed out of the harbor, feigning extraordinary difficulties, and when we got out into the bay I first sailed past an island to show him the osprey nest that had been there, and used every season by the same pair of birds, for at least ten years; it was made of large sticks and mud and was at least six feet wide and perched high on a promontory mostly surrounded by water. Ted said that he was not interested in birds that ate fish. The wind was coming up harder, I remember, but I sailed on toward the rocks at the mouth of bay to show Ted the harbor seals, which would swim to within a few feet of the boat and stick their heads up out of the water and look at us and then dive suddenly, sometimes passing under the boat. Ted said that he didn't give a damn about seals either and that he was beginning to feel sick and I knew I should have turned back, and as I think about it now I know that I was deliberately being a little cruel for all the times he had been cruel to me, and I sailed on out into the open Atlantic. The swells grew and the wind came up even stronger and I could see a line of squalls coming from the south, partly over land and partly over the ocean, and I told Ted that if we were lucky we might see a water spout, which he said would not be lucky at all, and I sailed on while

Ted begged me not to. I did turn back eventually, of course; I had wanted to time it so that the squalls hit when we entered the bay, but they came up faster than I had expected and we were still half a mile out when the rain started. We were in no real danger, but Ted was terrified. The sails snapped in the wind as it sometimes shifted abruptly, and the rain came hard. I loved it, and I intentionally heeled over until the lower part of the deck was actually running an inch or two in the water for a few moments and Ted was leaning back out over the other side screaming. I came around in good time, though, and when we entered the bay I ran with the wind, and there is nothing quite so wonderful as racing across the water with only the sound of the straining of the mast and of the bow cutting through the waves. I sailed all the way into the dock that day, not using the engine at all, and when we were tied up Ted leaned over the side and vomited. When his stomach was empty he still held on to the rail and heaved and when he finally stopped and I got him onto the dock he could barely walk. He would never go sailing with me again.

The rest of that Thanksgiving weekend I was telling about was bleak, and even my birthday could not bring me out of my depression, which was as exaggerated as my happiness had been a few days earlier. After I ran to the top of the hill that day I was telling about I ran the four miles to the Sound and stood for a while on the pier by the yacht club watching the waves, which did not look blue, as they had from the distance, but cold and grey. There were still a few boats moored in the harbor, empty and cheerless, unlike during the summer when there were parties on the boats or at least the activity of people cleaning and polishing and the sound of radios and often of guitars and sometimes even the sound of a violin drifting across the water, haunting in its simple, unaccompanied beauty, and I listened to the clamps clanking against the masts as the boats rocked in the water and to the whir of a winch pulling a boat out of the water at the club, and I was terribly sad. I was cold, I remember, and I did not feel like running back, but finally I did, and the run was difficult and unpleasant. I remember that when I got home I masturbated in the shower and thought about Ted, and when I got out of the shower I tried to call him again, but still there was no answer. I played the piano for hours that day, playing all of the slow, sad music I knew, and I began, for the first time, to work on the last three piano sonatas of Beethoven, which I had never had the patience to play before then (I had preferred the excitement of the "Waldstein" and the "Appassionata"), and which now, although I am still young—only 28—I love, particularly the last movement of the final sonata, which Beethoven called "Arietta," that takes a little melody and transforms it into something so sublime and transcendental that when it ends, very quietly, it goes on in your mind through the silence. As I write this I realize how much I have changed from the emotional and unreflective young man that I was then, and although, as I think I have said, it was not that long ago, it seems much, much longer, like a lifetime, and I think that the lengthening of my perspective of the time that has passed comes from the knowledge that surely within the next year I shall die. I do not mean this to sound maudlin or emotional; it is a fact, although not one that I have accepted without anger.

However, I am getting things out of order. (It is sometimes difficult these days to get my mind to focus on a single sequence of thoughts until it is finished and I do not know whether that difficulty is physiological or psychological, or both, but I know I hope that it is merely psychological.) That weekend that I am *still* telling about I played the piano for many, many hours, and I remember snapping at my mother once when she came into the room and told me that I was "moping around." I told her, I remember, that there was no such word as "moping," that it was slang, so of course Mother, believing strongly in the value of education, looked up the word in the *O.E.D.* and brought the appropriate volume into the living room and set it down on the piano with a thud while I was playing and read me the complete definition of the word along with its etymology. I have forgotten most of it, of course, but I remember that there was a long list of illustrious poets and authors, including Shakespeare, who used the word in one of its forms, and there were a lot of forms. I remember that one of the places Shakespeare used it was in *Henry V*, and later that day I looked up the passage and I still remember it: "What a wretched and peevish fellow is this King of England, to mope with his fat-brained followers so far out of his knowledge." (The parts of Shakespeare's plays I like best are the insults, and there are some very good ones. Sometimes Ted would roar them at me in fun, so I started reading Shakespeare, which I had never liked, just so I could retaliate.) *Mope* became my favorite word for a while after then, and it also became a joke between Mother and me, and whenever one of us was in a bad mood, merely saying "mopish" (my favorite, it means "stupidly bewildered"), or "moped" or "mopey" or "mopeful" would be enough to make us both smile, and although we did not use our little joke for a while when I first became ill because it made us both uncomfortable, now we use it again, although somehow it is different; we use it in a way that is lighthearted but with the knowledge of my illness and its inevitable outcome beneath that lightheartedness.

My birthday fell on the Saturday after Thanksgiving that year, and it was mostly a grim, cheerless affair. My parents took me to dinner at an inn that sat on the side of a hill that sloped down to the Sound, and although it was my favorite restaurant I did not enjoy much of the evening. My grandparents came, I remember, and throughout the meal they argued with each other about whether Grandfather should have been eating what he was eating—duck and red cabbage, I think—and

Grandfather argued with the waiter and Grandmother kept telling me that she hoped I'd change my mind and become a doctor until Mother finally told her to stop, saying, "Oh, leave him alone, it's his birthday," and then my grandparents, silent and sullen, both stared at my father with looks that meant to me, and to him, how can you let this woman you married talk to your parents like that, and I remember that my father ordered, and drank, a double scotch in the middle of the meal. There was a cake, of course, with candles, and waiters sang "Happy Birthday" while I felt like hiding under the table, and then there were presents, which my grandparents insisted I open there. As always, my grandparents gave me a wallet with one dollar in it for every year of my life—that year there were twenty stiff new bills in it—and a pen. (I think my grandparents have given me a wallet and pen for my birthday every year for at least ten years. I used to keep the wallets in a drawer at home, but now I just give them away again, and one year, a few years ago, I gave the birthday wallet to someone for Christmas and I forgot to take out the money before I wrapped the box and the friend I gave it to asked me if the twenty-three or twenty-four dollars was for something specific that he should know about.) My parents' gift that year was a total surprise, though. After I opened my grandparents' gifts, Mother handed me an envelope from her purse, which surprised me, because my parents did not usually give me gifts of money, but rather just gave me enough to meet expenses when I needed it. The envelope contained a large check and a note in my father's handwriting that said that he and Mother wanted me to have the independence to do things I wanted to do without having to ask them for money. I was moved by the gift, I remember, but then my grandmother saw the amount on the check and said, "Well, I *hope* you're going to give that back to your father to put away for you!" and we spent the rest of the time at the restaurant talking about money.

I certainly do remember the next day. My parents drove me back to school, and although I was trying to be polite they knew that I wanted them to leave so I could call Ted, so they went to my room with me but did not stay for more than a few minutes and then left and did not, as they often did when they drove me back to school after a vacation, take me to lunch. I remember that I walked with them back to their car and before they drove away Mother buzzed down her window and said to make sure that I went to class the next day, and I laughed and Dad smiled, and they left. I did not even have the patience to go back to my room to call, I remember, but called from a phone booth on the street. He answered almost immediately. "You're back?" I remember he said, and he told me to come down. It was a wonderful day. We made love and showered and made love again and showered again and went out for dinner—he drank too much, but I did not care—and then went back to his apartment and made love again, and the next day he missed work and I missed my morning classes and we stayed in bed and talked and drank coffee and ate English muffins, and made love, of course, and I remember that I did not ask him what he had done when I was away because, although I was curious, I was afraid that the answer might be something that would make me angry. I was right, of course, but I didn't find out until later.

Chapter 4

We were together most of the next two years and last year when we were together again we laughingly referred to those early years as the War Years. During the War Years we were often happy—sex was wonderful—but sometimes life was hell, and we finally separated with a dramatic fight that makes me smile to remember it now. When we were together again, when Teddy was sick, we often talked and laughed about the War Years, and Ted would paraphrase in as loud a voice as he could, which sometimes wasn't very loud at all, "That was the winter of our discontent, made glorious in summer by the sun in the Pines, and all the clouds that heaped upon our head in the deep bosom of the ocean lay buried!" and I would come in with, "Shall I compare thee to a summer's day? NO, thou art too bitchy!" and we would remember our fights (the fight that actually broke us up began in the Pines one Saturday evening, continued on the ferry, the bus, the train, and in a taxi in Manhattan, and finally concluded in glorious mayhem at one o'clock in the morning in this apartment) and we would remember our trips to Maine and all the good times we had, as well as the bad, and we were happy.

I don't remember many details of the time between Thanksgiving and Christmas that year we met. I know I was busy studying and Teddy had a small part in some Off Off Broadway play three evenings a week and was usually working the rest of the time, so often we just saw each other for sex; I would arrive late at night after he had just gotten home, we would have sex (that is not the same as making love) and fall asleep, and I was always up and out early in the morning, usually before Ted awoke. Sometimes he wouldn't let me visit, I remember, and I didn't find out until last year that he was occasionally having sex with someone else during that time and that he had spent all of Thanksgiving weekend with the same guy. He was sick when he told me, but it didn't make any difference: I slapped his face, in anger, and it was that spontaneous action that really brought us together again emotionally. After I hit him, hard, I was shocked that I had hit someone with AIDS and he was shocked that I had done it, but he was happy too because I wasn't treating him with deference or pity because of that damned disease, and after I hit him I started to apologize and he put his finger on my lips and all our differences and the five years we were separated fell away in an instant.

However, I am getting things out of order again; I was telling about December of the year we met, although there's not too much to tell between Thanksgiving and Christmas: we had lots of sex (Teddy had more than I did, it turns out); we almost never went out together because we were both too busy; and, oh yes, one day we met my father for lunch. I don't even remember where we ate, but I remember that Dad and Teddy acted as though they had known each other all their lives. They were both charming and witty and they told anecdotes from their youths and I had very little to say, and I remember that Teddy said to me during the meal, "What's the matter, dear? Cat got your tongue?" and I was really upset that he had called me "dear" in front of Dad, but Dad just laughed. Sometime during that lunch Dad asked Teddy to spend Christmas with us, and Teddy accepted. This was my father who had told me only two or three weeks earlier how disappointed he was that I was gay asking my boyfriend to spend Christmas in Maine with us? Now I laugh at it all, but then I didn't know what to say and I was *very* uncomfortable. (I should add that whenever Dad says he will do something he does it, and when he told me that Thanksgiving that I would always have his and Mother's support he meant it and he has taken an active interest in my life and has never been disapproving, at least not that I have known.)

Although there were some bad moments that Christmas, it was, as I think back about my life (what is this terrible thing that makes a twenty-eight-year-old think about his life as one who is sixty or seventy or eighty should?), one of the happiest times I ever had, and I could not tell this story without telling about it. Our family had owned the same house in Maine for more than fifty years, a large, comfortable old white house with a long, wide veranda in front, toward the sea. It was near the end of a point of land and, above a lawn that sloped down to the water, it faced a harbor and the town on the other side. When Grandfather bought the house, shortly after my father was born, it was a rustic, weatherbeaten building set alone in the woods. I have seen photographs of it then—fragile, browning, odd-sized prints that reflect the house as much by their condition as by the images they contain. Over the years Grandfather had owned it, before he sold it to my father, he had restored and improved it, preserving its original style and configuration while still making it tight and sound, and he had gradually cleared away most of the trees on the sides and on the slope toward the sea, so when seen from the water the house was surrounded by lawns and gardens, but since he had left the trees on the side toward the road, mostly tall, rough-barked old spruces that the Point the house was on was named for, from that direction the house was barely visible—only a peak of the roof and part of a dormer window could be seen. I am told that the tradition of going there for Christmas started four or five years before I was born when, a few days before the holiday, a tree uprooted by a bad storm fell against the house, destroying part of the roof and damaging the interior. My grandfather was called and he and Grandmother and my parents went up, expecting to have a cheerless holiday, but sometimes unexpected great surges of the forces of nature bring people together, and this storm brought my family—the summer folk—together with the year-round residents, and people my family had known only casually in the summer came to help. Men cleared away the debris with saws and axes, and a crew from a local boat-building works repaired the roof while their wives and daughters helped clean up the inside. They allowed Grandfather to pay for the materials but that was all, and in the winter along the Maine coast money was not then and is not now plentiful. Although the work was not finished, Grandmother declared Christmas Eve an Open House and, I'm told, forty or fifty people came, and the owner of the boat yard asked my family to come for dinner the next day and they accepted, and a tradition began that now, thirty years later, continues.

I was, as I said, surprised when Dad asked Ted to join us for Christmas that year, and I was even more surprised when Ted accepted, and I remember that, although I knew I would miss him, I really hoped that he would change his mind and not go, both because I was worried about how we would settle the question of where we would sleep—I was very uneasy about sleeping with, which I knew would mean having sex with, a guy in a room just down the hall from my parents' bedroom, but I knew that Ted wouldn't want to sleep in a separate room—and because I was worried about how I would introduce him to our friends in Maine, whom I had often heard refer to various summer visitors as "fags," "fairies," or "queers." I think Teddy knew I was worried about it, although I did not tell him, so of course he made a special point of insisting that he was coming, and he accumulated a pile of gifts for my family in the corner of his apartment, which worried me even more because I thought that my family would probably give him a token present or two but I did not think they would match his generosity.

Christmas that year was on a Friday, I think, and Teddy's play was over, so we drove up the weekend before so we could have a few days to ourselves before my family arrived. I had gone out to Connecticut the day before we left to get my car and had parked it in

the street on Ted's block, and when we came out early
the next morning a light, powdery snow was falling
gently. There was a thin layer of it on the windshield,
and I remember that when we were ready to leave Ted
brushed it off with his hand. I will never forget that
drive. We left before eight in the morning and we
should have been at our place in Maine by the late
afternoon, but after we left the city the snow became
heavier and, as we drove on, it snowed ever harder all
the way up. We drove the last forty miles at a crawl,
slipping around on the road with our headlights only
reaching out a few feet into the swirling white mass
around us, which seemed to be coming directly at the
car. Ted was frightened, I remember. He had grown up
in Hawaii and California and he had never been farther
north than New York in the winter. I remember he kept
saying, "Boy, if we get out of this alive I am going to
make myself the biggest martini you have ever seen."

We finally reached the town sometime around eleven
that night, I think, and we drove through it slowly, not
meeting a single car on the snow-covered street. We
could see lighted Christmas trees in the windows of
some of the houses and we both wanted to be inside
and comfortable, but then we were out of town and on
the way around the harbor to the Point and it was totally dark. The snow was several inches deep in the
road and there were no tire tracks and it was difficult to
see the road and stay on it, and I drove down what I
hoped was the middle of it looking over the steering

wheel with my head close to the windshield. I knew we weren't going to get through the long driveway that led to the house as soon as I saw it. I had called ahead and the drive had been plowed earlier in the day, but it was almost filled in and there was a drift beside it running out into the road. When I saw the drift I stopped and backed up and tried to get up enough speed to cut through it, but when the car hit the drift it slid and floundered and stopped, completely stuck in the snow. I spun the wheels, which did not help, and I remember that when I said we were walking, Ted, who didn't know where the house was, said he was afraid of getting tired and going to sleep and freezing to death, and he said that he wasn't going to get out of the car. I laughed and I told him that if it were day he would be able to see the house, and we each took a bag and set out in the dark; we had no flashlight. The snow was up to our knees in some places and I tried to play, scooping up some of the powdery snow and flinging it at Ted, only to have the wind blow it back over me, but Teddy was in no mood for fun. When we finally got into the house it was cold because in the winter it was kept heated to just above freezing, and as we stood inside and stamped snow all over Ted said he needed a Saint Bernard with a cask of brandy.

I have been trying to remember and reconstruct all the time that I spent with Ted as a final gift to him, and to myself, and there are many lacunae in my memory that I am usually only able to fill with great effort, although sometimes when I am showering or listening to music or playing the piano or talking to someone, not thinking about Teddy at all, suddenly I will remember some tiny fragment that I had not remembered before and then an entire incident or period of time will explode into my consciousness. However, some events I am able to remember clearly, in every detail, with no effort at all, like the time I took him sailing the summer after the Christmas I am telling about, or like the great fight we had on Fire Island that started one Sunday afternoon on the beach, continued in public at cocktail hour—Tea Dance, as it is called there—continued at our house, where I threw bottles of wine and liquor against the walls and followed them with plates of pasta, snatching Ted's plate out from in front of him as he started to take a bite, and finally ended when I went out into the night to get picked up so I would have a place to stay away from Ted and was brought to someone's house and had sex with all the six or seven guys there (and that wasn't even the fight that broke us up!).

That Christmas is one of those times I can remember clearly, without effort. We were so cold that night when we got into the house and we were hungry and tired, and Ted was in a horrible mood and I was worried about spending the next few days alone with him, but then I turned up the heat, although I knew it would take hours for the house to warm up, and we built a fire in the fireplace in the living room. I don't know why the sight, sound, and smell of a wood fire in a fireplace can

66

change even the bitterest or most awkward of times if not into times of good cheer then at least into times of quiet communal contemplation, but they do. (As I am writing this it is summer and sometimes even now, when I am feeling down, at night I turn the air conditioner on high and burn a small fire in the fireplace.) We built a great fire that night and pulled two rustic chairs made from whole pieces of trees—the kind of furniture often associated with Adirondack lodges, where in fact they had come from—up close to it and warmed ourselves and drank some scotch I had found. At first we drank the scotch straight but then, because the refrigerator was off and standing open and there was no ice, we drank it mixed with snow that we scooped off the veranda with our hands, and we sat with no light except that from the fire, which threw large, ominous shadows into the corners of the room. The house shook and creaked in the wind, and occasionally, when the wind died for a few moments and it was calm, we could hear the crash of the sea on the rocks. None of the beds was made and, although there were fireplaces in all of the bedrooms, we decided to sleep where we were and after we had several drinks I pulled out sleeping bags and pillows without cases from a closet and we moved the chairs back and rolled open the bags on the braided rug in front of the fire. We tried to zip them together, I remember, but we couldn't, so first we got into separate bags, still in our clothes, but then, unable to hold each other without exposing our arms and shoulders, we quickly stripped and squeezed into one bag and opened the other and put it on top of us. We were asleep within minutes.

We were awakened *early* the next morning—around seven I think—by a loud banging on the door, and I remember being half asleep and trying to shake Ted awake and to get myself out of the sleeping bag and then hearing someone open the door and come in and call out, "Hello!" I yelled that I'd be right there and pulled on my jeans, falling over as I did, which did awaken Ted, and I went out into the kitchen as I was buttoning my shirt and found the man who had plowed the driveway the day before, and who generally cared for the house when no one from the family was there, putting food into the refrigerator. We had a conversation that sounded something like this:

"Boy, you sure are up early this morning."

"Ye-up."

"I guess I didn't lock the door."

"Nope."

"I didn't get in until really late."

"That so?"

"It sure is. Driving was awfully slow. It took almost sixteen hours with only two stops."

"Ye-up. Good storm."

"Yeah, and I got stuck out in the road trying to get into the driveway."

"Ye-up. I saw." (There is a pause while I tuck my

shirt into my pants.) "Alice sent food. She figured you couldn't get to the store last night."

"Hey, tell her thanks for me, will you. I haven't eaten since yesterday afternoon and I'm starved."

"See ya got the heat up . . ."

And then Ted came into the kitchen with the opened sleeping bag wrapped around himself, which covered his shoulders and not much else, and he stood close behind me so that our sides were touching and there was a tremendous silence, as though a great chasm had opened in the middle of the room and we were leaning over it. I introduced Ted, awkwardly, and the man grunted out something between a greeting and a snarl and told me that we'd better get my car out, and he left, slamming the door on the way out. I ran back into the living room, I remember, and finished dressing as quickly as I could and went out into a totally white world, though still bluewhite, almost violet in some places, because it was barely light. The man had already plowed the driveway and had attached a chain to the front of my car and was waiting in his truck. It probably took no more than a minute to pull the car out of the drift, and when it was free he got out, unhitched the chain and threw it into the back of the truck, and got back in without saying a word. After I drove into the driveway he pushed the rest of the drift out of the road with a few slices of his plow blade and then he left, and as I got out of the car and went back to the house I could hear the rattle of the chains on his truck's tires receding, and when I was inside I had my first real fight with Ted. It started, I remember, when I told him he'd have to be a little less blatant than he was in the city, and I remember him saying, "You'd think he'd never seen a dick before," and we argued, of course, and then, as I was opening a can of coffee that the man had brought, I told Ted that I'd take him back to New York if he didn't behave, and then, as I plugged in the coffee maker, Ted took the can of coffee and poured it over my head, laughing as he did it, which made me really angry and I yelled and rushed at him and tried to tackle him—I have always had a quick temper—but he was, as I think I have said, both taller and stronger than I was and he held me off and then managed to turn me around so my back was toward him—and by then I was really fighting and yelling and calling him horrible names—and carry me back into the living room with his arms around my waist while I tried to break his fingers and then he kissed my neck while I tried to kick him, bite him, *and* break his fingers, and then he kissed me more and pulled my clothes off as I still fought, but he was laughing all the while and gradually I started to laugh too and then to kiss him back, and we lay down and made love on the floor. When we were finished we sat up and looked out across the snow-covered lawn, dotted with naked maples that had a line of white snow stuck to the windward side of their trunks and spruce trees whose branches were heavy with snow piled on the bowed boughs in fluffy, white, sparkling cushions, at the sea, which was the color of cold, gray steel. I remember I told Teddy that he was going to have to clean up the mess he'd made with the coffee and he said it had been worth it and I jumped on him and pushed him down and we made love again.

The following half week was the first time that we had had more than a day to ourselves, and I remember those brief few days that passed so quickly as one of the best times we had together during the War Years, and how I wish that we could unravel our histories since then and extend and spread out those few days until they filled the rest of our lives. I spend a lot of time now thinking about how my life, and Ted's life too, could have been different if . . . if we had not separated, if I had not gone to the baths, not that I necessarily blame going to the baths for this horrid disease, if I had not done countless other things that at the time I did them seemed insignificant but now, when I can see all of my life before and behind me as one large piece with finite boundaries, these actions that seemed so insignificant seem to have been crucial, life-determining or life-limiting actions. However, as I was recently asked by a straight friend, John, I have never thought about what my life would have been like if I were not gay. As I told my friend, with a vehemence and anger that surprised him coming from one who is dying, I *am* gay; it is impossible to imagine not being so, and I do *not* regret it.

However, I was telling about that wonderful Christmas in Maine. In the days before my parents arrived we shopped and decorated the house, buying a tree at a local gas station for, I think, five dollars, when the same tree would probably have cost fifty in New York, and we cooked for each other, and we made love, often. It was the way we started the day, and we usually made love at least once in the afternoon—once, I remember, after we put up the Christmas tree and before we had decorated it we made love with the pitch from the tree still on our hands and then later scrubbed each other's bodies in the shower with a sponge to get it off—but it was the evenings that I liked best. We stayed in a room that had been mine since I was a boy. It was on the second floor and overlooked the shore from above the veranda. And there was a stone fireplace across one end of it, and across the other were shelves that held, and still hold now, the treasures and memorabilia of a dozen summers—a large dried starfish that I had pulled off a rock near the place on the other side of the Point where I used to swim naked, pretty rocks that I had found and liked and kept, some smoothed by the sea and others, picked from rock piles or old stone walls, jagged and rough, a beaten-up baseball glove, a faded green knapsack with one strap torn off, a shelf of old, tattered Hardy Boys mysteries, a Monopoly set missing half its pieces and property cards and most of its money, a stack of jigsaw puzzles with notes taped to the boxes saying either "complete" or telling how many pieces were missing, and other things that I cannot remember. The bed was under the windows, and every night Ted and I built a fire and lay naked in bed, the fire giving the only light, and spent hours holding and touching each other, sometimes gently, sometimes with great strength, and always we made love, and sometimes when we were finished we looked out at the cold, moonlit sea through the reflection of the fire in the windows and did not talk. I remember how carefully I studied his body those nights, tracing with a finger the muscles in his chest and arms, the muscles that ran up the sides of his back and flared at the top, the muscles in his legs and thighs, and one night, I remember, when we had brought a bottle of red wine and a glass to bed with us, I traced the shape of the muscles with the wine and then licked it off. He liked that a lot, and it makes me smile to remember it.

All that week, wherever we went I had to beg Teddy to behave himself. He'd do things like grab me in the back of the pants as we pushed a cart down a supermarket aisle, grab my crotch as we walked down the street, or just put his arm around me when we were anyplace in public. I'd always slap his hand away and then he'd laugh and accuse me of being in the closet, and I guess I was a little then, unlike now when I am more militant, although it was later that week when I first publicly admitted being gay. Teddy had a great laugh, not a series of blasts but rather a contagious giggle that made his whole body shake, and I can remember being so angry with him after he had touched me in public that I wanted to hit him but at the same time not being able to keep from laughing myself. As I think I have said, I was quite worried about what would happen when my family was there, and my worry created tension between us that swelled and erupted into a fight the morning before they arrived, on the day before Christmas Eve. Teddy and I had never resolved the problem of where he would sleep when my family was in the house, although we had discussed it. I wanted him to move into another bedroom and he insisted that he wasn't moving, and that morning when we were getting bedrooms ready for my parents and grandparents I moved his things into the bedroom across the hall from mine while he was making the bed in the downstairs room my grandparents used so they wouldn't have to climb the stairs, which were steep and narrow. Teddy came up while I was making the bed in the room I wanted him to sleep in and asked me what I was doing, and when I told him he told me that he was sleeping with me and started to gather his clothes to move them back to my room. I started screaming at him and he didn't answer so I blocked the door, and when I wouldn't move he dropped the clothes in his arms and grabbed me and threw me against the wall so hard I lost my breath and my eyes teared and I slid down to the floor, leaning against the wall. He picked up his clothes and took them back to my room without speaking. When I was able to get up I went downstairs and pulled a chair up to the windows and looked out at the cold sea.

I sat there for a long time. I could hear Teddy doing things upstairs and then he came down and went into the kitchen and made a lot of noise. Finally he came out and told me that lunch was ready and I did not answer and did not look at him and then that son of a bitch (I use that affectionately) started kissing the back of my neck, which he knew I couldn't resist, and then we talked and he said that he wouldn't move into another bedroom but he said that he would behave himself around my grandparents and wouldn't tell them where he was sleeping and they'd never know if they didn't climb the stairs. I knew that was the best compromise I was going to get, so I agreed and we kissed a little—we used to do a lot of kissing—and went to eat lunch which, I remember, was canned tomato soup and tuna sandwiches. (Teddy could cook very well when he wanted to, and as I write this I wonder why he made such a dismal meal that day.) Of course, my grandfather decided he wanted to see the upstairs of his old house and climbed the stairs for the first time in three years and found us in bed, but that happened later.

The family arrived when we were still eating, I remember, and Teddy was a complete gentleman, holding Grandmother's arm on the steps and carrying in packages and luggage and asking about the drive up—they had taken two days so it would be easier for my grandparents—and generally being very gracious, which astonished me. He shook hands with my father and kissed Mother, who told him she had always wanted another son. Teddy's presents made a big pile under the tree and while he was out of the room Mother asked me where all the packages had come from and when I told her she said, "We have some shopping to do." I also explained the sleeping arrangements to her, and she said, God bless her, "Of course, dear," and I told her about our agreement about Grandmother and Grandfather and I remember she said that it was probably a good idea because, she said, she thought that Grandfather still advocated castration for homosexuals. I laugh as I write this, but I remember then it made me feel sick to my stomach.

Although it was, as I have said, a wonderful Christmas, it did have its problems. The afternoon my family arrived, after the car was unloaded and everyone ate lunch (Ted made tuna salad for everyone and Grandmother said she didn't eat tuna in the winter, but she ate it, and Grandfather asked for catsup in his), my grandparents took naps and the rest of us went shopping; Ted went with Dad and I went with Mother. I don't remember what Mother and I talked about, but I remember that we bought Ted two beautiful sweaters that had been knit in the area. One of them was a pale cream color flecked with purple and the other was a soft gray, and they both are in the closet as I write this. We bought some other things for Ted too that I don't remember, but I do remember that when we got back to the house Dad and Ted had already arrived and were sitting in the living room with Grandfather and there were more presents under the tree than I had seen since I was a child. Grandfather was drinking sherry and grumbling about the presents, saying something like, "Let's not forget that Christmas is Christ's birthday; it is not just for presents." I remember making some kind of exasperated expression at Teddy and then, to my enormous surprise, Teddy stood behind Grandfather's chair with his hands on its back and began quoting the St. James version of the Christmas story from Luke, the one that begins, "And it came to pass in those days, that there went out a decree from Caesar Augustus, that all the world should be taxed . . ." and Mother came into the room as he was doing it and stopped and listened and then Grandmother came in and stood by Mother and we all were quiet while Teddy recited, which, of course, he did beautifully. When he was finished we were silent for a minute and then Grandfather raised his glass and said, "A-men," and the little spell was broken. I remember that I gave Teddy a kiss, which Grandfather could not see, but Grandmother did and she stared at us hard. Last Christmas, when Teddy was so sick but insisted on going to Maine with my family and when Grandfather was no longer with us, I asked Teddy if he remembered reciting the Bible to Grandfather and he was quiet for a long time, lost in his own memories, but then he found the right thread and followed it and he said quietly, looking at me:

And it came to pass in those days, that there went out a decree from Caesar Augustus, that all the world should be taxed.

(And this taxing was first made when Cyrenius was governor of Syria.)

And all went to be taxed, every one into his own city.

And Joseph also went up from Galilee, out of the city of Nazareth, into Judaea, unto the city of David, which is called Bethlehem; (because he was of the house and lineage of David:)

To be taxed with Mary his espoused wife, being great with child.

And so it was, that, while they were there, the days were accomplished that she should be delivered.

And she brought forth her firstborn son, and wrapped him in swaddling clothes, and laid him in a manger; because there was no room for them in the inn.

And there were in the same country shepherds abiding in the field, keeping watch over their flock by night.

And, lo, the angel of the Lord came upon them, and the glory of the Lord shown round about them: and they were sore afraid.

And the angel said unto them, Fear not: for, behold,

I bring you good tidings of great joy, which shall be to all people.

For unto you is born this day in the city of David a Saviour, which is Christ the Lord.

And this *shall be* a sign unto you; Ye shall find the babe wrapped in swaddling clothes, lying in a manger.

And suddenly there was with the angel a multitude of the heavenly host praising God, and saying,

Glory to God in the highest, and on earth peace, good will toward men.

And when he was finished I had to leave the room so I wouldn't cry and Mother sat by Teddy and held his hand.

We had dinner that night (our first Christmas there, not our last) in a restaurant and I don't remember much about it. I remember that when we got back my grandparents went to bed and my mother and Teddy went upstairs, to wrap gifts I guess, and Dad and I sat in the living room in the dark looking at the lights on the tree. The piano there was out of tune because of the changes in temperature it was exposed to and because of the humid, salty air from the ocean, but nevertheless I remember that I sat down and quietly played a few Christmas carols, and then Dad said he had to wrap some packages so I went up to bed. Teddy had built a fire in the fireplace in my room, I remember, and when I got up there he was in his underwear starting down the hall to the bathroom. I pulled him back into the bedroom and hissed at him to put on some clothes, and after an argument in whispers he put on a pair of jeans and told me he'd get even with me later. We had fun that night; I can sure remember that. He kept tickling me, trying to get me to laugh aloud, so I squeezed his balls hard and he started yelling so I pressed a pillow over his head. We made love very quietly that night, on our sides, and we stayed awake for a long time.

The next day, Christmas Eve, is mostly blurred in my memory for some reason I don't understand. (I do sometimes wonder why parts of my memory are so fragmentary, why sometimes I can remember even the tiniest details of some event and cannot remember much at all about something that happened at almost the same time as the event I remember well, and I do hope that it has nothing to do with this damned disease I find myself with but I am afraid that it does.) Our Christmas Eve dinners in Maine always centered around an enormous pot of seafood stew, something like bouillabaisse, that contained several varieties of fish, lobster, mussels, scallops, shrimp, and all kinds of other good things. It never seemed very Christmasy to me, and serving it to guests in Maine seemed like the proverbial carrying of coals to Newcastle, but the stew was always good and the gatherings always friendly and cheerful. Mother seated Ted and me next to each other, breaking her usually inflexible rule that no one sat with the person they came with, and Teddy drank too much and he put his arm on the back of my chair and played with my back and neck and even tried to kiss me once or twice. I didn't let him do it, but Grandfather noticed and gave me a terrible look and as I tell this I wonder if that was the real reason he climbed the stairs the morning after Christmas and caught us in bed, but I am getting things out of order again. That night was bad enough. After dinner we all sang carols as we did every year, and Dad and I managed to improvise some pretty good four-handed piano arrangements, and it would have been a time of general good cheer if Teddy had not switched to scotch after dinner and drunk it in a large glass with only one or two ice cubes. As I think I have said, Teddy was an actor, and a singer, and when he had a few drinks too many he sang loudly, very loudly. That night he easily made more noise than the rest of us together, and eventually Grandmother said she had a headache and the party broke up early for a Christmas Eve. Teddy continued drinking scotch after everyone had left, and when I finally got him to come to bed he, of course, insisted on walking to the bathroom in his undershorts (white jockeys), and he had a very visible erection, of course, and of course he met my father in the hall. When he came to bed I tried to tell him that I was angry but all he wanted to do was fuck and he started slapping my legs, which made a lot of noise, so finally I let him have his way. We were not quiet; I think we moved the bed a good six inches across the floor.

I'm laughing as I write this, but I can remember that

the next morning, Christmas, I felt terribly embarrassed when I woke up and I didn't want to see my parents, who could not have helped hearing their son getting fucked if they had had their heads under their pillows and plugs in their ears (I admit it, I liked it). Teddy was sleeping soundly, of course, and I was listening to my parents move about and wondering if I could just stay in the room all day when my father pounded on the door and then roared out, "Merry Christmas, guys!" and then opened the door and said something like, "You two still alive?" and I do not think that I was ever as embarrassed as I was when I saw my father's grinning face that morning. When Dad went downstairs I got Teddy up and moving, and complaining, and eventually we made it down to breakfast, and I remember that Teddy proclaimed loudly that coffee had never tasted so good and Mother laughed. We spent most of the morning opening gifts, slowly, as Grandmother insisted, and Grandfather was very quiet and watched Teddy and me very carefully.

We went to our friends' house for Christmas dinner, as we always did, and my memory of that visit is that it was uneventful. Christmas dinner was always served at three in the afternoon, and we usually arrived around one, which gave the Old Folks—the parents and grandparents—plenty of time to gossip and trade news. By that year the Young Ones had grown up and I remember that Darryl, who was one of our host's sons and about my age, had received a pool table for a Christmas gift. All the Young Ones—there were six or seven of us—took turns playing pool before dinner, and boy, were Teddy and I ever bad at that wretched game, which first amused but eventually disgusted the others. I was glad when it was time for dinner, I remember. I don't remember much about dinner itself except that the main course was, as always, turkey, but I do remember that later, around seven or eight I think, all of the Young Ones went to a local bar together.

The bar is gone now, sold three years ago. Actually it's not gone, it's just completely different, with mirrors on the walls and a disco ball on the ceiling. The original, called the Pine Tavern, had been untouched for many years and had knotty pine walls and high-backed wooden booths with hard wooden seats, and it was a favorite gathering place for local youths, a place where those who had gone away to college after high school went during vacations to meet their friends who had found jobs and stayed in the area. The place was crowded that Christmas night and Teddy and I sat with a large group of people, some of whom I had not met before. Everyone was friendly enough; even though I was one of the summer people I *was* there in the winter and I was there with local friends, so Teddy and I were included in the conversations. Unfortunately, Teddy got drunk (his consumption of alcohol during the War Years was to be the cause of many fights) and started talking very seriously to a rugged-looking blond guy sitting next to him. Teddy would slide a little closer to the guy and the guy would move an inch or two away and then Teddy would move again, and I was sure there was going to be a fight. Well, there wasn't a fight, but there was quite a scene. Teddy excused himself and went to the bathroom and when he was gone the guy he had been talking to said to me, "Hey, is he queer or something?" and everyone sitting at the table became very quiet and waited for my answer. I'm proud of my response because it was the first time I was openly gay to strangers. I panicked at first and thought about lying, and then I told myself no I would not, and I said, "Yes, he's my lover." The guy who asked the question was stunned. "You're kidding," he said, and I said, "Nope," and then the guy on the other side of me, who had been a childhood playmate, reached out under the table and squeezed my leg. I was just twenty, you remember, and the juxtaposition of the confrontation and the secret touch from someone who certainly seemed straight (he died of AIDS two years ago) was too much for me, and I got up and got our coats and when Teddy came out of the bathroom I told him we were leaving. He didn't know what had happened, of course, and he said good-bye to everyone, and I remember that most of the people at the table, even some of my friends, didn't respond. When we were outside I told him about my public affirmation and the guy who had squeezed my leg and he laughed, and later that night we made love—quietly, thank God—for a long time.

We always slept naked and face to face with our legs and arms intertwined in ways that must have looked uncomfortable but were not to us, and we were sleeping that way when Grandfather opened our door the next morning and bellowed out, "What in hell is going on here!" I'd rather forget the next few minutes. Dad was out shopping with Grandmother, but Mother was home and she ran down the hall and tried to pull Grandfather out of my room. Grandfather, however, was not interested in leaving; no, not at all. While Teddy and I tried to wake up and keep ourselves covered Grandfather told me that I was a disgrace to the family and a cause of grief to my father and he called me a sodomite. Teddy, and I could have shot him for this with a good heart, said, "No, *I'm* the sodomite. *He's* a catamite." I thought Grandfather was going to have a heart attack. He roared out at Teddy, "The Bible says you should be put to *death*!" Now, if I had thought about it in advance of that moment I would have put my money on Grandfather in any argument with Ted, but I would have been wrong. Teddy, as he often told me, had become a gay activist when I was still learning how to masturbate, and he did not like being told that he should be put to death for being gay, so he calmly got up, completely naked and with his usual very impressive morning erection and, with his hands at his sides and his dick waving in front of him, backed Grandfather out the door, asking very politely if it was all right if we resumed the conversation when everyone was either dressed or undressed so that no one would have a psychological advantage. My poor mother. She turned away, trying not to laugh, but her shoulders were shaking, and after we heard Grandfather go downstairs we heard Mother whooping with laughter in her room. When Teddy came back to bed I remember that he said a little sodomy sounded like a good idea and although of course I protested—I was in shock—he didn't listen, and he was, I remember, very thorough. This sounds funny as I tell it, I know, and I am laughing as I write this, but it was also very sad. Grandfather never forgot the incident or forgave me, and he died three years ago without ever again speaking to me unless I spoke to him first, and even when he did speak to me he was very cold.

The rest of the day I am telling about was, as I'm sure you can understand, tense. Dad laughed when he heard the story, but he advised me to stay out of Grandfather's way, so I took Teddy up the coast to Pemaquid for lunch. We went to the Point in the afternoon, and I remember that the waves were huge, and when they broke over the rocks spray was thrown twenty-five or thirty feet into the air and then blown inland by the onshore winds. We stood as close as we could to the shore without getting wet, although occasionally an unusually big wave or strong gust of wind would send a spray of cold mist into our faces, and we put our arms around each other and kissed. I took Teddy out to dinner that night, I remember, and my family left the following morning. Teddy and I stayed two more days, enjoying each other and comfortable with our love (if you have not felt like this do not belittle those who have) and enjoying the beauty of the winter and of the sea, and we were very happy.

Chapter 5

As I have said, last year when we were together again, before Teddy died, we called the earlier years we were together the War Years. When we were first separated after the War Years we each made a great effort to avoid the other. I stopped seeing our joint friends and stopped going to bars or restaurants where I thought I might see Ted (I know now that Ted

did the same), and it was not until Wayne told me Ted
had moved to San Francisco that I returned to the
places and people that had been part of our life together. We did not see or speak to each other for almost five years, and during the beginning of that time
someone occasionally would try to tell me a piece of
news about what Ted was doing on the Coast and I
always said that I didn't want to hear it (although I
really did want to know), and then a year ago last
spring, after I had been trying to contact him but
couldn't, I saw him again. I was rushing into the Plaza
to meet someone for drinks—I had by then become, as
my friend Wayne said, a member of the Blue Brigade,
by which he meant the Wall Street types who wear blue
blazers to brunch on the weekends—and I bumped
Ted's arm as he came down the steps. I didn't look at
him and I didn't recognize him, and I apologized
quickly and went on. And then he called out, "Andrew" (it was the only time he ever called me that), and
I stopped and turned and looked and it was Ted, my
Teddy, although it did not look like him; his face was
thin and lined and there were black circles under his
eyes and I knew what was wrong as soon as I saw him.
I was nervous and embarrassed and awkward, and
when he shook my hand and said, "You look great," I
was so overcome by the change in his appearance that I
could not say anything and I was silent for a moment
and then finally said, "Are you all right?" He laughed a
little and said that he had just lost weight, and I held

his shoulders and pushed him back at arm's length and looked carefully at him and then I noticed that he was wearing makeup, and I rubbed a little of it off on my finger and held my hand out to him palm up. I knew that people with KS used makeup on their faces to hide lesions, and I looked at Teddy's eyes and Teddy looked at the makeup on my finger and then that son of a bitch turned away and started to leave, and when I grabbed his arm he tried to shake it loose. I remember I yelled at him, "Where the fuck do you think you're going!" which attracted the attention of people going in and out of the hotel and embarrassed him, and he said, "Leave me alone," and tried to turn away again, and when I said I wanted to talk to him he said, "I don't want your pity."

I was different than I had been during the War Years: then I had been young and usually easily controlled by Ted, but last year I was older (twenty-seven) and more mature, and very confident, and that day I stood up my date and held Teddy's arm tightly and steered him around the corner and pulled him down the block and sat him down at a table at the outdoor cafe at the St. Moritz. It was one of those beautiful late spring days when a warm breeze sweeps up the coast and over the city from the south and the air, even in Manhattan, smells sweet and clean and people carry their jackets in their hands and smile at the world, and it was on that beautiful day in that beautiful season that is an annual reaffirmation of life that Teddy told me he had

AIDS. He'd had Kaposi's sarcoma for almost two years and then, a couple of months before we met again, a bout of *Pneumocystis carinii* pneumonia. It took a long time to get the complete story from him and a couple of times he started to cry and once I did, and he kept saying again and again that it was so good to see me, and then he'd say, "But I don't want your pity." He was right, partially; I think part of what I was feeling *was* pity, but I was unsure of what to say—I remember trying to avoid mentioning or even alluding in any way to dying—and I was uncomfortable because he was an old lover, and also because he was the first person I knew with AIDS who had been more than a friend. After I finally got the story out of him he said he was tired and had to go, and that spring day, overriding all his protests, I took him to his home in a cab and went upstairs with him, and when I saw that dreadful little room he lived in and the filthy bathroom down the hall I told him he was coming back to my apartment with me, and of course we fought about it.

I'm getting things out of order again, I know, but I am sitting here at my table this beautiful day in early September and somehow the beauty of this day made me think of that day I first saw Teddy again and made me want to write about it; however, I know I'll return to this later. Before I interrupted the story I was telling about that Christmas in Maine that Teddy and I spent with my family, eight years ago this coming Christmas and, as I said, my family left first that year and Teddy

and I had a couple of days to ourselves before we had
to leave too. When we finally got back to the city we
went directly to his apartment, and I remember that I
brought my luggage up, only intending to stay until the
dorms opened. I never really left after then, until that
May, at the end of the semester, when I used some of
the money from my father's birthday gift to get a larger
apartment for us. Teddy kept his apartment too, but
after then he lived with me most of the time.

That first spring I lived with him was not very peace-
ful, but I did love him and sex was great. The fights,
however, were not great. He did three things I could
not stand: he played moronic disco music at deafening
volume most of the time when he was home; when he
drank he almost always got drunk; and when he was
drunk he tried to pick up other men, even if he was out
with me. His drink—his "drug of choice," he called
it—was a very dry Bombay gin martini, which always
tasted like straight gin to me, and I can remember coming home and hearing the stereo pounding as soon as I
came into the building—he lived on the fourth floor—
and walking up the steps knowing Teddy was going to
be drunk and then coming in to find a half-empty gin
bottle on the table and Teddy dancing shirtless in the
middle of the room with a glass in his hand. I would
yell at him to turn down the music, and sometimes he
would turn it down a little, but other times he would
ignore me and keep on dancing, so I'd turn it down
myself and then sometimes we'd fight or else after I

turned the music down I'd go into the bedroom and shut the door, and then Teddy'd crank it up again. Sometimes when we fought about the music in the late afternoon he'd say, "I'm going to fuck the hell out of you," and he'd throw me down on the bed and do just that, and then afterward we'd get dressed and go out to dinner, and sometimes when we fought we wouldn't speak to each other for the rest of the evening.

I can remember one particular incident very well. It was a Friday night, and when I came home we had a drink or two and made love, and then Teddy wanted to go out. We argued, of course, about where we would go because he wanted to go to the Anvil, which I wanted to avoid because I'd had sex with many people in its back rooms and when I was out with Teddy I didn't want to meet anyone I'd once had sex with. We finally compromised on the RamRod, which I didn't want to go to either because I'd had sex with several men I'd met there, but at least I'd never actually had sex on the premises. Teddy, I remember, dressed in full regalia, with black leather pants, a black leather bomber jacket (it hangs in my closet as I write this), a black leather cap, army boots, and a red *and* a blue handkerchief in his back left pocket. I wore my usual blue jeans, dress shirt and sweater, and a blue pea coat, and I remember that we attracted quite a bit of attention when we entered the bar. In fact, because of my preppy appearance we attracted more attention than a man who was leading another man around by a chain around his neck. Whenever the man holding the chain stopped, the man wearing the chain would squat on his haunches at his trainer's side, and when the man holding the chain wanted to move he gave the chain a hard yank and the man on the other end stood and followed and then squatted again when they stopped. I had never been much interested in the S and M world, but Teddy found it very exciting and, as I found out last year, even during the War Years while we lived together he continued to have sex occasionally with partners who were into heavy S and M. That night I am telling about the thing I had feared most happened, and someone whom I had gone home with saw me and came over to talk. I didn't remember his name, so I couldn't introduce him to Ted, but I do remember that the guy said something to me like, "You don't remember my name, do you?" and when I admitted that I did not he introduced himself to Ted and shook his hand and I do remember that he told Ted that I was a "hot number." Of course, Ted wanted to know the details, and the details were, in this case, to use one of Teddy's favorite words, "sleazy." I had gone home with the man, who had used me to satisfy himself and then shared me with his apartment mate *and* a man who lived across the hall. Teddy found this very exciting, and he asked for very specific information, which the man provided gladly, enjoying my embarrassment, and then that son of a bitch Ted, and this time I do not use it affectionately, asked the man to come home with us. I'm not going to tell much about the rest of the evening because I'm sure an accurate telling would make even strong-hearted women faint, but I will say that the evening involved the use of toys (not jacks or alphabet blocks, either) and it was then that I found that I really did enjoy what is usually referred to as S and M. (I know the term and this account is much too general, but prudence and a desire to preserve some privacy even when I am no longer living, when this will be read, prevent me from being more specific.) I can also remember several things about the next morning (the other man left during the night): I remember being stiff and sore; I remember being embarrassed; and I remember that Teddy was unusually sweet and caring. He took me out to breakfast and I also remember that I told him that I had enjoyed the activities we had participated in but that I did not want to have any more threesomes, and he agreed, although of course he didn't mean it.

I realize that I've gotten off the track a little again; before my digression I was telling why we didn't go to gay bars or clubs together very often. The first reason was, you remember, that I didn't like meeting people I'd had sex with. The second reason was that when Teddy got drunk, and he usually got drunk when we went out, he often tried to pick up strangers, even when I was with him. There are many stories I could tell from that spring I am now writing about, but because I do not want this to be solely a sexual biography and autobiography I'll only tell one more, about something that happened late in that spring about a month before we went to Fire Island together for the first time. We were out somewhere I didn't want to be (Crisco's, I think), and Ted had taken a Quaalude and was very drunk and I wanted to leave and he wanted to stay and, of course, we fought, and he poured a drink down my chest and thought it was very funny. I didn't. I was very angry, I remember, and I left him there and went down to Badlands and managed to get a seat at the bar and got thoroughly drunk myself. I don't remember what time I got home, but it was very late and when I came into the apartment the bedroom door was closed and sounds of sex were coming from inside. I kicked the door as I went by, I remember, and then tried to go to sleep on the couch, and I remember that Teddy came out and asked me to join him and I refused, and then he went back into the bedroom and the guy he was with came out and *he* asked me to join them. I was very rude, and I remember that I went to sleep to the sound of steady, rhythmic slapping. I didn't speak to Teddy for the next several days, and I slept in my underwear on the edge of the bed as far from him as possible.

There were good times during the War Years too, of course. Although we did fight often, we were happy a lot too, and when we weren't fighting life could be great. We always walked everywhere, and usually hand-in-hand, which drew lots of attention that, truthfully, we enjoyed, and when we slept, when we were not fighting, we turned in toward each other and slept face to face, each feeling the other's breath, mine on his neck, his on my face, and as I write this I can almost feel our arms around each other. School went very well that spring I am telling about; I made excellent grades and I played the piano better than ever before. That was the year I learned to play the *Goldberg Variations* well, although my interpretation of them was, I think now, much too romantic, with too much pedal and rhythms that were too flexible. It seemed that everything I played that spring went well, and I attributed that to being in love. I remember convincing Teddy to come up to the practice rooms to hear me play, and about halfway through the *Goldberg Variations* he began to whistle, something else of course, so I stopped and told him he was rude and we argued a little, of course, and when I finished the piece, I remember, he asked me if I knew anything with a better beat to it, so I played the Prokofiev *Toccata* and he liked that just fine. We never did share a love of the same kind of music—he skipped my recital my senior year, which caused a fight, of course—but last year when he was living with me again he'd listen quietly when I practiced and gradually he started asking me to play specific things, and in the weeks before he died he asked me to play Schumann's *Kinderscenen* again and again, and now I play it often for myself and think of him, and the piece has become for me not only scenes from my childhood but scenes from my entire life.

That was also the spring that I started going to a gym

regularly to lift weights. I had been a good swimmer and runner and was strong and hard, but Teddy wasn't satisfied; he said I wasn't realizing the potential of my body (his words). I agreed to go to a gym reluctantly, not because of the physical difficulty but because I had very little time. On the advice of a friend, who said lovers should never use the same gym because if you break up not only do you not have a lover but also your body goes to hell, I joined a different gym than Teddy belonged to (though I thought that we would never break up), and although I complained about the time it took I was diligent about it and I liked the way it made me look and feel, and I continued to work out until last year when I became so weak. In fact, during the years that I was separated from Teddy the gym became an important part of my life. I saw the same group of people at the gym that I saw in the Pines in the summers and, in the early eighties, at the Saint on Saturday nights during the winters, and we all thought we had everything gay men could want—health, beauty, friends, almost limitless hot sex—and when we first heard of AIDS we thought that we were invincible; it could not strike us. It did, though. I remember so clearly going to visit Sean, a friend from the gym—it was in the fall of '83—and closing my eyes when he showed me the lesions scattered across his washboard stomach and magnificent pecs that had been the envy of everyone. Sean also had a thick dick that reached, it seemed sometimes, halfway to his knees, and I can remember another friend from the gym telling me before Sean got sick, as we watched him going into the shower, that he'd die happy if he could just have a couple of 'ludes, a gram of good coke, and one night with Sean. But Teddy and I knew nothing of this that spring I am writing about (1979); we had not heard of AIDS, and even if we had heard of it we would have thought that it could not harm us.

I took Teddy to Connecticut a few times that spring to visit my family, and the visits were uneventful. I showed him the town and we went out to old favorite places of mine, which he said were "too damned straight and too damned preppy," but there were, thank God, no major embarrassing incidents that I can remember, and we participated in that great suburban ritual, Shopping, which involves spending hours driving from store to store and looking for parking spaces. During one of our visits Grandfather wanted to talk to Mother (Dad was away that particular weekend) and, because he knew Ted and I were there, he stayed in his car and blew the horn until Mother came out. I went out too, to say hello, and I remember that he would barely speak to me and would not look at me. (As I think I have already said, he remained hostile for the rest of his life and died without forgiving me.) Our last visit to Connecticut that spring was to pick up things my parents were giving me for my new apartment, and I remember thinking then that our lives—Teddy's and mine—and our life together, would last forever.

I'm sure that everyone feels the same way when they move into their first apartment, or house, after leaving their parents' home, as I did when I moved into my first apartment that spring, where I still live and where I am writing this. When I rented this apartment I had no furniture, other than the little my parents had given me, and Teddy and I went out and bought everything in one day, including a piano (while I tried different instruments Ted kept telling me to hurry up), with my money, of course arguing about everything—he said the things I liked were "tacky"—and then that night, back at his apartment, we drank much too much Champagne. It was a week or so, I remember, before everything was delivered, and I had to admit that Teddy's selections had been right, and I remember telling him so and him saying, *"I know that."* After the big things came we spent another day buying sheets and towels and things for the kitchen. And food! We bought enough staples to open a bakery and a restaurant, and we bought a bottle of every kind of spice in existence, I'm sure, and some of those bottles are still in the cabinet and mostly untouched (I guess I should throw them out). Teddy moved quite a lot of his stuff in too, including, unfortunately, his stereo, which meant that we had two of them in a one-bedroom apartment (he put his in the bedroom), and most of his clothes. I remember one night in early June when we were finally finished with the apartment and we drank Champagne to celebrate and looked out across the city as dusk came and the sky darkened and lights came on until finally it was night, and then we had dinner by candlelight. A year ago June, when Teddy was back, we sat and watched darkness come to the city on an almost identical evening to the one years before, and although we did not mention it we both, I knew, remembered the earlier evening, and then when it was time for dinner Teddy asked for candles but we still did not speak about the time we were both remembering. Later that night, however, we did reminisce, and that was the night, which I think I've mentioned, when, in the course of an argument, Teddy told me about some of his sexual infidelities from the War Years and I slapped his face.

Somehow that first summer we were in this apartment Teddy manipulated me into taking a share for the two of us on Fire Island, in the Pines. He had asked me about going to the Island in the summer several times that spring and I had always said no because I knew I was going to be taking courses and I also wanted to go to Maine, as I had done almost every summer but, as usual, Teddy listened to me and then did what he wanted to do anyway. He found the share through a friend of his who went to the same gym, and in early June he presented it to me as a *fait accompli*, telling me that his friend, Wayne, had a bedroom that he couldn't fill and would be stuck for the extra rent himself because he had signed the lease. Therefore, Teddy said, he had had to take it and if I didn't want to go out, I didn't have to. Of course I wouldn't let Teddy go out to the Pines every weekend by himself (I *was* young, *and* naive, but not *stupid*), so I said I'd go, and of course there was one little detail that Teddy hadn't told me about: money; he had only paid a quarter of the cost. However, I said I would pay the rest of it, and I did, and we did take the share. I will never forget my first weekend in the Pines. It was in mid-June, and we didn't go out until Saturday afternoon, and I walked into a house that was literally shaking from the volume of the music playing and was filled with the most beautiful men I had ever seen, all mostly naked and all doing something with feathers. They were preparing for a party that evening and almost as soon as we arrived Teddy left with someone to try to borrow a pair of *pumps* for himself, and he left me in this house full of men making costumes out of feathers, smoking pot, and drinking rum. To say I was surprised would be an understatement; flabbergasted might be more accurate.

I think there are several stages in "coming out" (as I write this I wonder where the phrase "in the closet" came from, anyway): first, you realize that you're gay, which could be quite an upsetting discovery I think, although it wasn't for me (you come out to yourself); then, eventually, you work up the courage and tell someone, and then you gradually tell lots of people, hopefully including your parents, and *then* you go to the Pines and find out what it's all about, and what it's about, I've decided, is, at least partly, style, and in '79 and '80, the summers I was there with Ted, there sure was a lot of it. It was a gay paradise; everyone was either young and beautiful, bright, or rich, and a lot of men there were all of these things and more. It was depressing. At the beginning of that first summer I really didn't fit in. I wouldn't wear costumes; I didn't like to use drugs; I didn't like crowds; and I always felt as though I was being evaluated, which I hated. Teddy, however, the bitch, acted like he owned the island. He knew *everyone*, and wherever we went people would stop us and talk and Teddy sometimes would introduce me, and sometimes he wouldn't which infuriated me, and then after the person we were speaking to had moved away he would whisper some little bit of sexual information to me—"Beautiful, but the Lord gave him a three-inch cock," "There's room in that ass for a Cadillac," and "He's not so pretty when he's in the sling at the Mine Shaft" are three I remember—and I would always say, "I don't want to hear it," but Ted would say, "Of course you do," and keep right on talking.

I did go to the feather party that first night I was there and I did not wear feathers; Teddy went and he did wear feathers. Somewhere he found this tight, dumb-looking, mid-calf-length, low-cut gray dress, and he clipped apart a pink feather boa and sewed (yes, *sewed*) it around the bottom and around the neckline, and completed his costume with black pumps, a ridiculous blond wig, and long, trashy, glittering earrings, and, oh yes, scarlet, *bright* scarlet, lipstick. I was, as Grandmother says, mortified, and I remember pulling

him into our bedroom and telling him that I wasn't
going anywhere in his company when he looked like
that, and he said that he'd just have to find someone
else to take, and I was sure that he'd do it, so of course
I went, dressed in blue jeans, sneakers, and a Lacoste
shirt (I remember one of our housemates telling me,
"Alligators were *last* summer, dear"). I don't remember
much about the party except that I was overwhelmed. I
was nervous so I drank too much of some awful red
punch too quickly and then, because I had had too
much to drink, when someone offered me some cocaine
I took it (a first) and then Teddy told me I was too hyper
and he gave me a pill, a Quaalude I found out the next
morning, and I took that too (another first). I do remember dancing with my shirt off, which I never did
find, but I don't remember much else. It seems that I
almost had sex on the dance floor with at least a half-
dozen men, and behaved, by any standards, out-
rageously. For the next couple of weekends almost everyone I met on the Island talked to me about that
damned party, either to tell me they had seen me or,
worse, heard about me.

Fire Island wasn't all fun, though. Teddy and I had
our first big fight there. I guess it had been coming for a
long time. I was interested in a one-man monogamous
relationship, but Teddy, who had been on the gay
scene for a long time (he was only five years older than
I but had been going to the Island since he had been
seventeen) found it boring. He liked me well enough

but, as he told me last year, during the War Years he found my possessiveness—clingingness, he called it—oppressive, and as I write this seven years later I can see that I was not very understanding and I was certainly very immature. I can remember that fight well. It was a hot, clear Saturday in July, the kind of day when the sun makes the skin feel hot after just a few minutes of exposure, and Teddy went to the beach early in the afternoon to work on his tan line (having a tan *line* was more important than just having a tan) while I stayed at the house and studied because I had an exam on the following Monday. I worked for a couple of hours and then went to the beach myself and I remember standing at the top of the steps over the dunes looking for Teddy's bright orange towel, and I remember seeing one but passing over it because it had two people on it who were laying face-to-face with their arms around each other and then, some fraction of a second later, I realized it was Ted with someone else. I stood there for a few minutes watching as the two of them nuzzled and cuddled, and then I went back to the house and made myself a gin and tonic and sat on the deck, burning in the sun and burning with anger until I could stand it no longer and I ran down the walk and over the steps to the beach and ran to Ted's towel and kicked sand at them and screamed a string of foul names at Ted, and people nearby applauded. There was going to be a big party that night, and I remember screaming at Ted that he could take his little trick to the party because I wasn't going, and then while he yelled, "Wait! Wait!" I ran back to the steps and then to the house, where I picked up a shirt and some money and left quickly so he wouldn't find me there.

I must have looked like a fool. I went west on Fire Island Boulevard, the walk that goes past the harbor and through the center of town, crying openly, sometimes walking and sometimes breaking into a run for a block or so, until I reached the end of the Pines and then I turned toward the sea and walked on the beach toward Cherry Grove, still crying. I had stopped by the time I reached the Grove, but I still must have looked awful because when I reached the Monster one of the bartenders, an older man, said to me, "My dear, *what* is wrong? Whatever it is, we'll just make you a little drink and make it better," and he filled a glass with gin, added a thimbleful of tonic, and put it in front of me. The Monster in the Grove was and is a wonderful place, and last summer was the first summer since the summer I am writing about that I didn't make it there for a visit. That earlier summer, in the late afternoons, the bar was staffed and the customers entertained by two bartenders who could not be less alike: one, a man of indeterminate age but probably around sixty the summer I am telling about, and the other, a young hunk of a man who, if I remember correctly, and I may not, had once been a truck driver. The two of them could have taken their show on the road. That afternoon after the older one asked me what was wrong I told him, and then he loudly told the younger bartender, and everyone else in the place, "Oh dear, he's had a fight with his boyfriend," and then the younger man gave me some obscene advice that had something to do with shackles and piercing that made me laugh. I stayed there drinking gin and tonics for two or three hours and finally I was convinced to go find Teddy to, as the older bartender said, "kiss-and-make-up and make babies." I was in no condition to walk back down the beach, of course, so I took a water taxi and got out at the harbor in the Pines.

There is a great Saturday evening ritual in the Pines called Tea Dance, or Tea by the cognoscenti, although it has very little to do with tea or dancing. No, instead it is a time when everyone gathers after the sun has gone down but before it is completely dark to have a few drinks, perhaps share or score some drugs, to look at everyone else, and to gossip (Teddy was, as I think I have said, great at gossiping—he knew some little piece of dirt about everyone). Tea was going full blast when I arrived at the harbor that afternoon and I could hear the music and the din of hundreds of voices, and I knew Ted would be there so I went to find him. I didn't see him at first and, after I got a drink, as I pushed my way through all the beautiful bodies looking for him, someone grabbed my arm and asked me if I'd seen Ted yet. His tone held a significance beyond that of an ordinary question, and I was almost afraid to say no, but I did and the guy turned me around by the shoulders and pointed, and there was Ted, that son of a bitch, making out in a corner with the young man from the beach. Once, during the years we were apart, a friend told me that the next thirty seconds were my finest moments. I pushed my way through the crowd to Ted and tapped him on the shoulder and, when he turned toward me, said, very quietly, "Slut," and threw my drink into his face. The crowd around us fell silent; no one moved except to part to give me a path out. Then Ted's little friend began to tsk and wiped Ted's face off with his shirt, and when I saw that I stopped and held out my hand to a stranger, who handed me his drink without speaking, and I turned back and threw that drink into Ted's friend's face, and everyone started to talk at once and I left quickly.

I was halfway home when I heard Teddy running behind me and calling me to wait but I did not even slow down, and when he finally caught me he grabbed my hand and I pulled it away and walked on without speaking while he told me he loved me and that he was sorry, and gradually I began to walk more slowly and to listen and then to respond a little and we walked to the sea and walked along the beach and although I was still angry I tried to overcome it. When we got home everyone was out, at a party, and I fixed some pasta for us while Ted rolled a joint and smoked it and then, as I put a plate in front of him and went back for my own Ted decided that he had to tell me everything so he told me that he had gone to his little friend's house after I had seen them on the beach and had had sex. Twice! I think it was the twice that set me off again. I grabbed some bottles of wine and liquor on the counter and threw them against the wall behind Ted's head, but Ted was so high he just laughed and kept on eating so I grabbed the plate from in front of him just as he was taking a bite and threw it against the wall too, followed it with mine, and then ran out. I had not had sex with anyone but Ted since I had met him (other than the one threesome that I have already told about) and that night I was determined I was going to get even, and boy did I. I went to the woods between the Pines and the Grove that is called, affectionately, the meat rack, and went home with the first man who asked me. His housemates were all up when we got to his house, I remember, and they gave me some drugs and then someone took me into a bedroom and left the door open and eventually everyone in the house joined in. I slept there, I remember, but it was light before I did.

It was after noon before I made it back to the house, and I remember having the same feeling in my stomach you have when you are a child waiting to see the dentist as I stepped onto the sundeck. I opened the screen door as quietly as I could, I remember, and I found Wayne scrubbing the walls. No one else was there, and I went into my room and pulled my duffel bag out of the closet and began filling it with the things from my drawers, and soon Wayne came in and sat on the bed and watched. Neither of us said anything for a while, and then he asked me what I was doing, and I told him I was going to Connecticut for a few days to give Ted time to get his possessions out of my apartment. Wayne didn't say anything for a while longer but just lay back and watched. He was, and is, a beautiful man. He has the body of a gymnast, the smile of a model, and blue-gray eyes the color of smoke that rises from an outdoor wood fire in the fall when the wood is slightly damp, and, he is modest. He has become a close friend, a "sister," as he says, and now I see him often. Sometimes he comes over and cooks dinner or sometimes we order food to be delivered, or sometimes he just comes to talk.

However, again I am getting this out of order. That summer that now seems so long ago Wayne asked me why I was leaving and at first I didn't say much and then it all poured out. I couldn't find a single nice thing to say about poor Teddy: I complained about his music, his drinking, his drugs, his infidelities, his mistreatment, and everything else I could think of, and Wayne listened and nodded and didn't say anything until I was finished. I can remember him sitting there then, nodding, and saying, "Sounds rough," and then, after a pause, asking me if I'd like to know what Teddy had said about me the night before. I can remember that first I said, "I don't give a damn!" but then I said, "Oh, all right, what?" and Wayne said that Teddy had been crying and had said that I was a spoiled little WASP who wanted being gay to be just like being straight except that I had sex with men instead of women. Then I was quiet, and after a while Wayne said, "Well?" and then, after more silence, "How about a vodka and orange juice?" and I said yes. We sat on the sundeck and drank our drinks, not saying much, and I remember that Wayne asked me if I loved Ted and I said I didn't know, and there was some more silence and then he said, "He loves you, you know," and there was still more silence and then Wayne said, "He said to tell you he's on the beach." "Shit," I said, and I put down my glass, and Wayne leaned over and gave me a kiss. I went to the beach dressed as I was, not changing into swimming trunks, and I can remember that as I walked down the steps to the beach I wondered what I would say. Teddy was lying near the steps with the rest of the housemates, and when I reached the bottom one of the housemates saw me and waved and then they all got up at once and left their towels; only Teddy stayed and he watched as I approached. I stood beside him as he lay on his towel and neither of us spoke for a minute or two and then I said, "Well?" and Teddy, that bastard, reached up and gave my crotch a hard squeeze. I laughed and he pulled me down and we kissed and hugged and generally made a spectacle of ourselves. We were back at the house, making babies, as the bartender at the Monster said, within twenty minutes.

Things were all right for a while after then. I began to be more comfortable on our weekends in the Pines, forcing myself to participate in all its great rituals until one night, while dancing shirtless with Teddy at the Sandpiper with a bottle of poppers in my hand to "Could It Be Magic," which the DJ had resurrected, at least for the evening, I saw, as if for the first time, the beauty of Teddy's sweaty chest under the lights, and I looked at the men around me and realized that we were all beautiful, a great crush of muscles covered with smooth, tanned skin, of hair limp and dripping with sweat, of glistening upturned faces following the heat rising in the air; we were *humanity*, and not just that, but *gay* humanity, and in that room there was a magic that made us feel as though we were one. For me it was like coming out of a dark tunnel into the light to realize that I was a part of all that beauty, and I took a hit of the poppers and in its rush threw back my head and sang out, "Baby I want you . . ." and Teddy pulled me to him and kissed me and then released me and sang too, and Teddy and I, and all of us, were one in the music.

I can remember that night so clearly. The disk jockey brought us higher and higher until we were all exhausted and it seemed as though we had to stop and rest, but still he led us on, playing faster and faster music, and we followed until, when it was light, he led us into unrestrained frenzy with a phenomenally fast "Boogie Woogie Dancing Shoes," and then he let us down easily and the music stopped. Everyone had felt the magic and there was a great cheer when he stopped playing and the lights came up, and there was long applause, and then someone started stamping on the floor and soon everyone in the room stamped in rhythm, and when the lights went back down we all screamed together. If my memory is correct, and I think it is, he played only three more songs. He started with a funky piece called "Hot Butterfly," which has a bass line that makes standing still impossible, and when we were all dancing again he abruptly, without mixing, switched to a disco version of "The Man I Love," which is much faster, and then, finally, he played "Could It Be Magic" again, and again the room overflowed with love and beauty, and then, when we all wanted more, the DJ stopped the music abruptly, not fading it out but cutting it off in the middle of a phrase, and again we all screamed. But the DJ would not relent; it was over. Teddy and I walked out into the morning and walked back to the house along the beach and the sun, low in the east, was reflected so brightly from the still sea that the reflection was painful to look at, and along the beach behind us and in front of us were men, usually couples, walking home, separated by long spaces as though we were all beads tied at fixed points on some long string that was being pulled slowly toward the horizon. I remember I said to Teddy, "This is so beautiful," and I remember clearly Teddy saying to me, "Yes, but it won't last forever," but I thought it would: last forever. We went back to the house that morning and got towels and then went back to the beach and slept on the sand.

That August I took Teddy to Maine again. We had the house to ourselves for a few days and I had hoped that we would find the same mood that had been there at Christmas, but we did not. Perhaps it was because the town was full of people and we were not isolated, or perhaps because the newness of being lovers had worn off; I do not know. I remember that the Saturday night we arrived we went to a bar that was only open in the summer and was mostly patronized by gay tourists, and we both said that being there was almost like being back in New York. We were tired, and a little down, and we started talking about what our housemates in the Pines would be doing and then, both being a little intoxicated, I admit, we called the house on Fire Island from a pay phone in the bar, collect. Everyone there was getting ready for a party, I remember, and when we hung up Ted tried to convince me to drive back, immediately, and I almost agreed. However, I did love the sea, and I had the use of a sloop for a week, so I convinced Ted to stay, and the next day I took him on the sail I have told about already. He got very sick, as I have said, and he was very angry, and for the next few days he spent most of his time getting drunk and pouting. One of my aunts from Boston was using the house starting in the middle of the week after we arrived, and Ted said he didn't want to share the house with strangers so we left, driving up the coast to Mount Desert Island, where I was going rock-climbing. I had hoped that Teddy would climb with me, but no, he wasn't climbing any cliffs, he said, so I spent the days climbing with my climbing instructor and then, when I was exhausted and wanted nothing but sleep, I would go out to bars with Teddy. I did not want to be on the side of a cliff when I was hung over, so I drank very little those nights, which offended Teddy, who began to say what was to become a litany over the next year, that I thought I was better than he was, and so of course one night we fought, and of course that night I drank a lot, and the next morning while climbing I had to lean back on my anchors and turn my head to the side and vomit. It was a horrible climb. We left for New York the next day.

The rest of that year seemed uneventful as I was living through it; there were holidays and birthdays and good times and arguments and I was working hard at school and applying to grad school and Ted was working hard and was in two short-lived Off Off Broadway plays (not at the same time), but it all seemed so normal, although we did fight a lot, that I was really stunned when the break came, even though its immediate cause was my fault. However, when Teddy and I talked about that year when we were together again he told me that I had changed dramatically, and as I think about it now I know that it was true. Before then I had been gay, of course, but only in that I preferred to have sex with men instead of women; gay culture did not touch me, and if it did I scorned it. I had had sex with many men, as I have said, but Teddy had been right, I did think I was somehow better than they were: *I* wasn't in the gay ghetto; *I* didn't dress like a clone; *I* wasn't effeminate (not that being effeminate is equivalent to being gay); I was not interested in what I considered to be *their* petty little world. And then do you know what happened, I became part of it, and I could not get enough. Life for me, at the time I met Ted on the steps of the Plaza last year, had become a complicated landscape of parties, gyms, beautiful men, knowing the right people—the *in* people, going to the opera, the symphony, the ballet, rushing off to the Island in a seaplane in order to make Friday Tea. And I do not apologize for that; it was an interesting and satisfying way of living and one that I miss. And it all began that first summer Ted took me to the Pines. At the beginning of that summer I seldom drank, I didn't take drugs, and I didn't much like to dance; but by the end of summer I loved them all. I remember that our last weekend in the Pines that year was at the end of September and the house was empty. We had all cleaned the house and moved our things back to the city the previous weekend, but I wanted to go out just one more time. Ted wasn't interested, but I can be very persistent when I want to be and I managed to convince him to come with me, complaining all the way, of course. It rained heavily all weekend, and we kept a fire burning in the fireplace continuously. Most of the stores and the Botel were already closed, with their windows boarded, and Teddy just wanted to stay inside by the fire and read some new play he was interested in and cuddle, but I wanted excitement. That Saturday night, after going to a sparsely attended Tea where everyone wore heavy sweaters and jackets and still shivered from the cold and which was sad because it was the final one of the season and everyone was saying good-bye, and after eating cold sandwiches back at the house with Ted, I went out alone in the heavy rain and walked the board-walks, looking for life, music, a party. I eventually found one, and I stayed there, drinking, taking drugs, and dancing until morning. When I got back to the house I found Teddy sleeping fully dressed on the couch, which he had pulled in front of the fireplace. He was very quiet when he woke up, I remember, not so much angry as sad, and we left the Island under dark skies, chilled by a cold wind.

We were both very busy that fall, which was my se-nior year. I was working hard at school and preparing for a recital and still finding the time to swim and to work out at the gym, and Ted was rehearsing for a new play and also working hard at his job. We fought a lot, I remember. We sometimes fought about drinking. I thought that Ted drank too much (although he never drank when he had to work) and when I told him so he would accuse me of thinking that I was better than he was and tell me it was none of my business and drink even more. I learned that there was nothing I could do when this happened, so I usually just went to bed and was sometimes roughly awakened later when Ted decided that he wanted sex. We began fighting about clothes too. He would wear my sweaters or jackets without asking, which I did not mind, but he was very careless with them and often ripped or soiled them, and once, after he had somehow managed to rip a hole in the sleeve of my favorite leather jacket I got irrationally angry and swung at him with my fist. I missed him and tried to grab him at the same time he brought his hand up, and his fist collided with my eye and broke the skin. There was a lot of blood and we were both shocked and Teddy was very sorry, although it really hadn't been his fault because he hadn't intended to hit me, or at least not that hard. Two days later I had an ugly black eye, and I remember that we had been invited to a black and white party that I wanted to go to, but Teddy convinced me not to go because he said he didn't want people to think he had beaten me up, and besides, he said, it was a black and white party, not a black and blue one. In early November that year I gave a recital at school, and I played, among other things, Schumann's *Symphonic Etudes* and *Kinderscenen* and Scriabin's *Vers la Flamme*, a powerful piece that pulls the listeners in until they are in the midst of an apocalyptic conflagration at its end. I had also programmed the Gershwin *Preludes* because I thought Ted would enjoy them but, of course, Ted didn't come to the recital. I remember waiting for him to come backstage at intermission and then looking for him afterward and not seeing him and being very disappointed. My friends at school wanted to take me out for dinner to celebrate, I remember, but I declined and went home alone. Ted wasn't there either. He came home about four in the morning, smelling like sex and, of course, we fought, and of course he denied that he had had sex with anyone, and it wasn't until last year that he told me that he had met someone in the subway on the way up to my recital and gone home with him. In the subway!

There were a lot of pleasant times too, though, and I remember them fondly as I write this. We really did enjoy doing domestic things together: cleaning, shopping, doing laundry (Teddy said that the attended laundromat in our block wasn't careful enough and didn't use hot water so we did our laundry ourselves), and even arranging flowers. Ted was a great cook and I was a terrible one. I remember that I had always thought that scrambled eggs had to be cooked for fifteen minutes or so, and one of our first mornings in this apartment I made my fifteen-minute scrambled eggs for Ted, who took one bite, got up from the table with his plate, took it into the kitchen, threw the eggs into the trash, and told me I was taking him out for breakfast. After then he taught me to cook. He bought several good cookbooks, which are still in the bookshelf as I write this, and once or twice a month we would make a grand, sometimes very complex dinner together, often inviting Wayne and his boyfriend of the moment or one of two of the other housemates from the summer. These were fine times, and last year we occasionally did it again, and poor Teddy looked forward to those evenings so much. They seemed to bring him back to health for a few hours, and if you did not look at him but only listened you could believe that it was the old, healthy Ted talking and not someone who was seriously ill.

That year we went to Connecticut to visit my family every couple of months, but because of my grandfather we did not spend the holidays with them. We cooked our own Thanksgiving dinner and invited all our gay friends who were staying in the city to share it with us and to celebrate my twenty-first birthday too. It was quite a party. Some people came early in the afternoon and helped with the cooking, more arrived for dinner, and still more came for dessert and drinks after their dinners somewhere else. Everyone helped clean up, and then I played show music on the piano and everyone sang. We made a lot of noise and late in the evening John, the straight man who lives in the next apartment with his girlfriend, Patty, knocked on the door and asked, not too pleasantly, if we would mind doing the music from *The Fantasticks* since he could hear us anyway. We invited him in, of course, and he brought Patty and they stayed until the party was over, and the next day they sent us flowers with a note that said it was the best party they had ever been to. (Since then they have become good friends; they helped me take care of Teddy when he was sick, and now they help me out too.) That Christmas Ted and I had dinner together at the Edwardian Room at the Plaza. I remember that first the maître d' seated us at a terrible table near the door and as we drank martinis Ted got angrier and angrier saying, loudly, that he didn't see why one had to have blue hair to sit by the windows. I was afraid he was really going to make a scene, and so I said I'd talk to the maitre d' and I did, and I also gave him two $20 bills, and he gave us a table in the Fifth Avenue corner by a window. When I told Ted how much I'd tipped, Ted started saying, again loudly, that we shouldn't have to "bribe" the help, but I managed to get him quiet. I missed Maine and my family, but I did have a good time; it was a different kind of Christmas; a gay Christmas with the man I loved. It makes me laugh to remember that Teddy gave me, among other things, a set of tit clamps, a dildo, and a pair of handcuffs without the key (he kept that on his key ring).

I don't remember much about that spring. We fought sometimes, of course, but it didn't seem any more serious than usual. We both continued to work hard; I was accepted into Columbia's M.B.A. program for the fall, which made Ted taunt me about being a preppy; we went to lots of parties. We didn't seem to have as much sex, but we didn't have as much time together either. I graduated from Columbia that spring, and although I didn't want to go to commencement my parents and grandparents wanted me to go, so I agreed. Teddy, however, would not go and when my family took me out to dinner afterward and invited Teddy too, he wouldn't go to that either. I remember that I expected that he would either be out or would be drinking and drunk when I got home, but he was neither. He handed me a glass of Champagne—Dom Perignon—when I came in the door and led me inside by the other hand. The apartment was beautiful. There were exotic flowers everywhere—hundreds of dollars worth in huge arrangements that Teddy had made himself—and the only light came from dozens of candles whose soft light was reflected in the shiny black ebony of the piano and diffused by the flat white walls. I remember the shadows of the flowers on the walls, and I can remember so clearly how handsome Teddy looked in that light and how good it was to hold him, and how fine it was to make love with him later.

That summer we were staying in the same house in the Pines with most of the same housemates and I remember that as summer approached I was very excited about going to the Island again, and of course it was something for us to fight about. I had the entire summer free because I was not working or going to school, and I intended to spend most of it in the Pines. Ted, however, could only come out for the weekends, and he wanted me to stay in the city with him during the week. After many long discussions, when I assured him that I wouldn't trick when he wasn't there, we compromised, and I agreed to spend every other week in the city. How different it was going out for the first weekend that summer: The summer before I had not wanted to go and had known no one and was shocked by the feather party the first night; that second summer I couldn't wait to get there, I knew several people on the train, I sat on the ferry with friends from the previous summer and gossiped with them, and one of the first things I asked when I reached the house was if there was a party anywhere that night. I remember everyone told Ted, "You'd better watch him," and I laughed. Teddy didn't.

The fight that broke us up happened in early August and although its immediate cause was definitely my fault, things had not been going well with Ted all that summer. I spent every other week in the Pines and Ted had to go back to the city on Sunday nights, and he was convinced I was having sex with other people while he was back in New York. I wasn't (in fact, I know now that *he* was having sex when I was alone on the Island). However, every time I walked to the ferry with him when he was on his way back he would be insulting and abusive about what he thought I was going to do while he wasn't there. As I tell this it seems that one could wonder why we even stayed together as long as we did or why I still think about him and write about him, and the answer to that is, as trite as it sounds, that I always loved him. In the years we were apart I tried to hate him, but often I would find myself thinking about him and missing him and then when I realized I was doing it I would become angry at myself, and I often dreamed of him too, tender, sexual dreams that left me feeling sad and lonely when I awoke and remembered them.

However, as usual I'm getting things out of order.

The great fight that broke us up (now it makes me smile to think about it) happened on a gray, wet Saturday afternoon. Ted wasn't coming out until five or six in the evening and it was too cloudy for the beach and I didn't feel like staying in the house, so in the midafternoon I walked to the Grove to visit the bartenders at the Monster. Only the older bartender was there when I came in (now I know his name is Sherwood) and there was only one other customer, a darkly tanned blond young man with deep blue eyes who was so beautiful it was impossible not to stare at him. He was wearing only gym shorts, and everything about him was perfect—muscular thighs, small waist, ripply tummy, the works— and I tried to look only at the bartender or out the window but again and again I found myself looking back to this beautiful man, who was, I thought, only a year or two older than I. Finally the bartender said, "Oh, do you two know each other?" and then, when he saw that I was embarrassed, he said, "Now don't be shy," and he introduced us. The guy's name was Alex, and he moved to my end of the bar and the three of us talked, complaining about the weather, I remember, and then when I went to the bathroom Alex followed me a minute or two later and offered me some cocaine (he kept the little bottle in his jockstrap), and I accepted it. It was fabulous stuff and over the next hour I took a lot of it. By that time it was probably four o'clock or so, and I wanted to get back to the Pines to meet Ted and Alex said he lived in the east end of the Grove, toward the Pines, and that he'd walk part of the way with me. It was sprinkling when we left the bar, I remember, and when we'd walked a block or two it started pouring heavily and Alex said, "Come on," and ran to his house and I came in with him. It was a mistake. I won't tell the details, but of course we had sex, and more cocaine, and it must have been after seven before I left. The rain had stopped then, and Alex went outside with me and gave me a big kiss, just in time to be seen by Ted, who had been told by Wayne that I was at the Monster and had come to look for me.

What a night! Ted immediately started screaming at me, things like "slut," "whore," "tramp," and Alex ran inside his house and slammed the door. Ted and I walked down the beach screaming at each other, to the amusement of passersby, but when we reached the Pines we agreed to a truce so we didn't fight in front of the housemates. Everyone was leaving for Tea when we arrived and they convinced us to go with them. It was a mistake. We stood in different parts of the room and didn't look at each other and then, after we'd both had several drinks and I was talking to someone I'd met during the previous week who Teddy didn't know, Teddy cruised by me and hissed, "Is he one too?" The guy I was talking to retreated quickly, and it angered me that Ted had intimidated him, so I called Ted a drunk and he threw his drink at me, and then I threw my drink at him and ran out with him following me. I thought he was going to beat the hell out of me and there was a ferry tied up at the dock so I ran on it, and of course Ted followed, yelling insults, and on the ferry across the bay, on the taxi to the train station, on the train across Long Island to the city, and in the taxi uptown, we argued in tight whispers that sometimes erupted into angry, loud voices, sometimes squeezing the other's leg until it hurt or working an extended knuckle into some sensitive place in the other's arm or between the ribs.

The end came, ridiculously enough, over stereos. When we got home Ted went into the bedroom and put on one of his acid rock records and turned the volume up painfully high. I retaliated in the living room with the Immolation Scene from *Götterdämmerung*. Neighbors pounded on the walls. I could stand it no longer and I kicked open the bedroom door and grabbed his turntable and threw it on the floor, then his amplifier, then his tuner. It made a horrible noise, and he watched without moving, amazed. Then he pushed by me and went into the living room and did the same to mine. He kicked through the front of my speakers too. I was so mad I thought I might take a knife and kill him so I left. I told him I'd have the police throw him out if he was there when I returned, and I spent the night in the baths. He was gone when I came back the next morning. He had moved all of his things out the night before except his turntable, which was in the trash, and he had left a photograph of himself on the bed. It was a beautiful photo I had taken one morning when he was just awakening, naked, face-down, holding a pillow, vulnerable-looking, and when I looked at the photograph I cried and then I called him. We fought on the telephone and he hung up without saying good-bye.

Chapter 6

I had never spent much time in the baths, but that August they were my home. I did not go back to the Island that summer, not even to pick up my clothes, and I didn't want to go anywhere I might see Ted, so I spent those long, hot August nights in the baths, slippery with sweat in the arms of strangers, moving to the music, euphoric with drugs, going out into the heat of the morning swaying with exhaustion and drunk with sex. The best times were Sunday nights, when waves of beautiful men would come back from the Pines or the Grove frustrated from a weekend that was often necessarily nonsexual because they were sharing a room with several other people or because they had taken too many drugs or just because often there is not time for sex on Fire Island, and I would welcome those men gladly and enjoy each one for what he could offer for fifteen minutes or half an hour and then I was anxious for the next man, and if no one came to my room I would walk the halls and if I did not soon find some hot, young muscular beauty I took someone older, overweight, or unattractive, and when I propositioned one of these latter men I could see the surprise in his face and hear it in his voice, and it was these men whom I tried hardest to please, and I enjoyed not only the sex itself but also my partner's enjoyment of it, and as I think back about those times I realize that some of the hottest sex I had was with men who were not what is commonly called "hot," yet they *were* hot and their passion was completely sexual and nonnarcissistic; making love with them was not, as I think it sometimes is between two gay men who are physically beautiful, like making love to oneself.

That fall I began to repeat the life I had had before I met Ted, working hard at school during the day and then spending the evening hunting for men, no, for sex, in the parks, at the docks, in empty trucks in the meat packing district where the sidewalks were slippery with animal fat, in the baths, and wherever I looked I found what I wanted. I did not go to any bars or clubs at first because I did not want to see Ted, but then one Friday in October, when I went to the baths early, around five, to catch the married businessmen who stopped in for an hour or two—and a man or two—before returning to suburban domesticity, I saw Wayne, who was there for the same reason. He came up behind me in the hall, I remember, and pulled my towel off, and I turned around, furious, because even in the baths, where everyone knew that everyone was there for sex and there was no pretense of anything else, there were standards of conduct: you did not grab a stranger in the hallways, although a soft caress was acceptable if it was not indicated in some way—a gesture, a look away, a gentle push with the hand—that the touch was not welcomed; if you were rejected you did not protest or, worse, beg, and you left quietly (I remember once when I walked into a dark room and put my hand on the stomach of the man lying there he said, "No thanks," and, unaccustomed to being turned away, I stood beside him in surprise with my hand still on his stomach and he suddenly screamed, "Get out!", and I was so embarrassed I left the place immediately and didn't go back to that particular bath house for several weeks); in some bath houses you did not engage in particularly loud or violent activities (although there was an establishment where a can of Crisco and assorted paraphernalia were accepted as an ordinary part of one's baggage); if you saw someone you knew who obviously did not want to be acknowledged you looked away; you brought your own poppers. So I was very angry when someone pulled my towel off from behind and I turned around ready to fight, and it was Wayne. I grabbed for the towel and I remember he held it away from me and looked up and down my body and said, "Nice." I laughed and he gave my towel back and went to my room with me and we sat side by side cross-legged on the bed and talked, and he told me that Ted had moved to San Francisco. I remember I said, "Good," but even then I didn't mean it. I also remember that Wayne and I tried to have sex that night but it was a ludicrous failure because we both wanted the same thing, and when we realized this we both laughed and Wayne said, "Back to the halls," and he said he'd call me, and we parted friends. Later that evening he saw me going into a room with a black man (in the years Ted and I were apart I developed a politically incorrect desire for black men with large penises, which I may, or may not, tell about later) and he flashed a thumbs-up sign at me and I laughed. Wayne did call, and we became good friends and dancing buddies—sisters, he calls it—and we even had sex occasionally after an evening of dancing, and we still are friends. (He's coming for dinner tomorrow, and I'll show him this paragraph—I hope he can read my writing.)

That fall, after Wayne told me that Ted had moved to

California, I returned to the bars and often I could be found at the Anvil or at the Mine Shaft, where I sometimes waited in line for my turn in the sling, and I was determined not to fall in love again so I never went home with anyone or brought anyone home with me, and then something unexpected happened. I had almost totally abandoned the piano that fall, spending my free time swimming and working on my body instead, and if I did practice I did it at home, and one day, probably in late September, when I was sitting in the sun on the steps of the library with my shirt off, a young woman named Diane, whom I knew slightly from the year before, sat beside me and told me that she had been at my recital and that she had enjoyed it. We talked about music, I remember, and I told her I didn't play much anymore and she was very flattering and told me that I should never give it up. We talked for quite a while and then, when I had to leave for class, she asked me if I'd like to have dinner with her, and from the way she asked I knew the request was made out of more than a desire for companionship. I was very surprised I remember, and I blurted out, "I'm gay, you know," and then she was embarrassed and said she'd always wondered if I was and said why was it all the nice guys were gay, and then *I* was embarrassed. We did have dinner a couple of nights later, in an Indian restaurant, and it was an awkward time. We talked about Indian food and ordered and then there was silence and then I said that I had played a few of the *Goldberg Variations* that week and Diane seized that topic, and we must have spent close to an hour talking about the proper tempos (she thought they should go much slower than I did then, although now I enjoy playing them so slowly there is sometimes a noticeable silence between notes) and about how much ornamentation should be used. Diane was much more of a musical scholar than I was and knew a lot about the structure and historical perfor- mance practices of the *Variations,* but she did not have as much keyboard technique as I did, and I remember that she asked me to play the *Variations* for her with her tempos and ornamentation sometime, and I also re- member that after dinner that night I told her that I was meeting someone and she told me to have fun. I wasn't meeting someone, however; I caught a cab and was wandering the halls of the baths, wearing only a towel, within thirty minutes.

Diane called me about a week later, I remember (I had given her my phone number when she asked for it because I couldn't think of a reason to tell her why I wouldn't), and asked me if I'd like to have dinner again and I agreed, and we had dinner together almost every week for the rest of that fall, which was clear and warm and bright and filled with a new crop of beautiful fresh- men whose casual self-confidence sometimes made me just stop whatever I was doing and watch and want to touch them. Diane and I always went to restaurants and often it was an early dinner so I could later go to the baths or bars, although I told her it was because I had to study or because I was meeting someone. We became good friends (she was the first close woman friend I had in my life) and we talked about being gay and straight and about the importance of sex in one's self-identity, and I remember she often repeated the same thing she had said that day we spoke on the library steps, that all the nice men are gay. I didn't think it was true then, and I don't think it's true now, when two of my closest male friends are straight (my cousin Daniel, and John, the man who lives in the next apartment), but I do think that many straight men lack simple kindness and compassion, or perhaps not lack it but just hide it somewhere. (Wayne said after he read this that straight men are not as concerned with the pleasure and happiness of others as gay men are, but I don't think I believe that either.) Diane, however, could not be convinced otherwise, and I remember when I suggested to her that she might be gay too she said she'd tried sex with a woman once and that she found it "disgusting." We talked about this often too, and I gave her some lesbian writing, which she read and dismissed as irrelevant and self-indulgent, and we argued about that, and she jokingly tried to convince me that I was straight, and our weekly dinners continued.

I went home for Thanksgiving by myself that year, and it and my birthday were sad, grim affairs. My parents wanted me to tell them all the details about Ted, but I would not (they were so wonderful when I brought him home again last year, treating him like a long-lost and much loved relative), and when I got back to New York that Sunday I remembered how happy I had been the year before with Ted and I cried. I called Diane in the middle of the afternoon and asked her if she wanted a drink, and we met at a bar near her apartment, which was near Columbia, and I told her all about Ted, which I had not done before, and then we started to walk, and at a traffic light I stopped and took her hand and looked into those green eyes of hers and knew something was changing. We walked for a long time, first to Rockefeller Center to watch the skaters and then up to the Park, where we took a ride in a carriage. After that we walked back down Fifth Avenue, and we didn't talk about much, I remember, but just watched the people—the sidewalks were filled—and finally I asked her if she wanted to come to my apartment for dinner. We never did have dinner. When we got here she asked if she could try the piano and I opened a bottle of wine and watched her play, and then she asked me to play something for her, but instead I brought out an arrangement of Tchaikovsky's Sixth Symphony for piano duet and we played it together. It is a terribly trashy arrangement, but it was a lot of fun to play and we both worked hard and concentrated and when we were finished we realized that we had made that horrible old arrangement sound as good as it possibly could. I certainly will never forget the next few minutes. We sat beside each other on the bench and talked about the music, and then Diane said suddenly, "Do you want to fuck?", not "make love," but "fuck." I almost fell off the bench, and I said, "No!" She said, "Why not?" I said, "I'm gay." She said, "Shut your eyes; you won't know the difference." I said, "Oh yes I will," and then she said to me, "If it's warm, wet, and moves, what do you care?" and I laughed so hard I had to lie on the floor.

Our affair lasted until the spring, when she graduated. It probably would have ended soon anyway because, although I liked her, she made me realize even more strongly than I had before that I *am* gay and I *like* being gay. It was a crazy year, though: I had sex with Diane once or twice a week but I still cruised the bars and went to the baths, and then later I told her about the men I had met and what we had done, and she was very interested. I remember she asked me once if I would invite a man to come home with me so she could watch us have sex, and I said no, emphatically, so she took herself to a theater that showed gay pornography. When she told me about the movie she saw she said it was "interesting," and she had lots of questions about how things felt. As I tell this I wonder where she is, and I do hope, I pray, that I did not give this horrible disease to her. We lost touch several years ago. She went to graduate school in Chicago the year after I am telling about and we wrote to each other for a while and then one of my letters came back stamped ADDRESSEE UNKNOWN: RETURN TO SENDER and I never heard from

her again, although I still live at the same address. I
remember last year I told Ted about her and he laughed
and said some insulting things about me being a bisex-
ual, which I'm not, and then after he'd teased me for a
couple of days he admitted to living with a woman, and
having sex with her, for almost a year a few years before he had met me. When Wayne was here for dinner
a couple of months ago I told him about Teddy's bisex-
ual period (he already knew about mine), and Wayne
claimed he was the only "pure" gay man he knew because he'd never had sex with a woman. It was nice to
see him that night. I played some tapes of the music
that we had all danced to in the Pines in 1979 and '80,
and he asked me if hearing that music didn't make me
very sad, and I said no, I am happy to have lived
through those wonderful times, and I am. My answer
made Wayne very quiet and I thought he was going to
cry, but the bad moment passed after a while. I don't
want people to cry for me, I want them to live and be
happy, and sometimes these days I get very impatient
with people who come to visit and feel that they can't
mention the words "AIDS" or "death" or "dying" or
even talk about something too far in the future. Hell, I
have AIDS, I *am* dying, and the result *will be* death, and
pretending otherwise is a waste of the time and energy
that I still do have.

However, I realize that of course I've gotten off the
track again, and I guess I've gotten a little angry too. I
get angry easily these days, not so much angry at any

one or any*thing*, although I'm sure the government could do more to prevent and to cure this horrible disease than it's doing, but just angry in general, and how different that is from those years I am telling about when I was filled with happiness, when everything—a returned glance in the street, a caress in the baths, crossing Great South Bay to the Pines in the moonlight, life itself—was a joy. I remember that the year I broke up with Teddy Diane went to her home for Christmas break and I did not want to go to Maine so I spent Christmas alone in New York, spending the day, which was warm and rainy, walking the streets looking at Christmas decorations and store windows and finally ending up in the Village outside a gay bar where the colored lights in the windows were reflected from the wet sidewalk, and when I went into that bar and the bartender said Merry Christmas I was as happy as I've ever been in my life. There was a little tree with flashing lights sitting on the bar, and as I sat beside the tree and talked to strangers, all of us drawn together by a powerful feeling of brotherhood, of sameness, I again thought, as I have so many times, that there cannot be a finer thing than to be a young openly gay man in this wonderful city. I went to the baths that night, I remember, and I didn't have sex but instead spent a couple of hours talking with someone who was in New York visiting his family and had left his lover home alone in Pennsylvania. The guy's parents didn't know he was gay, and when he came into my room, after the usual question, did I want company, he sat down and the first thing he said was, "Do you have a lover?" and I remember how sad I felt when I said no and then how surprised I was that I was sad. I asked the guy, whose name I don't remember, the same question and he said yes, and it was like a dam breaking, and he told me about his lover and his family and after we'd talked for a long time he asked me if I'd like to have a drink with him, and I said sure and we got dressed and left and went to a straight bar across the street and then later shared a cab uptown, and I was content. It was a beautiful Christmas.

The next two years are not very distinct in my memory; although I can remember incidents and boyfriends and flawless days bright with blazing suns that melted into clear nights aglow with starlight, I cannot put everything into an accurate order, and it is not because of this disease but because I lived such a frantic life then, driven by a desire to succeed at school and in my first job, and driven by a desire to extract every last bit of joy, of pleasure, from my life that I could. I went to the Island in the summers and I remember torrid days when the ocean was glassy and came in to the shore in languorous swells, when I would lie on my towel for an hour or two and then get up and walk lazily along the beach, sometimes stopping to dig my toes into the wet sand below the high tide line, sometimes walking just above the water so that occasionally a wave would wash over my feet, and always looking at men, nodding or

speaking to people I knew, smiling at strangers. Sometimes when a stranger smiled back I waved and did not
stop, but sometimes I would stop and talk and then we
would walk on together. Sometimes in the late afternoons I would walk on the boardwalks just to look at
the houses and the people in them, and occasionally I
would see, indistinctly through a filter of leaves, two
naked men embracing under an outdoor shower, and
the sight of two beautiful, tanned men caught in the
sunlight in a private moment would catch my heart and
I would be awash with unexplainable sadness. I swam
too, sometimes long, lazy swims straight out to sea until
the people on the beach were small and far away, and
sometimes, for exercise, fast, hard swims parallel to the
beach. When the shadows grew long and the bright
sunlight diffused into dusk I would always be found at
Tea, where once I had felt out-of-place and uncomfortable but by the time I am thinking about I knew everyone, or at least it often seemed that way.

Sometimes at Tea I would, as I guess a politician
would say, work the room, speaking to everyone I knew
and sometimes introducing myself to a beautiful or
handsome stranger, and sometimes I just sat with my
arm around one of my housemates, watching the crowd
and wondering at the abundance of beauty. Sometimes
after Tea I would return to the house for dinner and
then go to my room and lay naked on my bed with the
doors toward the sea slid open and feel the cool breeze
on my body and abandon myself to the comforting wash

of the waves and eventually sleep. More often, however, I would go back out and dance until I met someone I liked and spend the dawning hours in a euphoria of sex, and I can remember that those nights when I didn't find anyone I wanted, and I walked back home alone along the beach, the sight of silhouettes of couples against the water or against the sky at the top of a flight of steps made me terribly sad. On one of those nights there was a full moon which made a streak of silver on the water, and I stripped off my clothes and walked out through the surf following the reflection of the moon. I swam out a long way, enjoying the feeling of the water and the cool moonlight. I swam mechanically, without thought, and then, after an unknown amount of time had elapsed, I was surprised to find myself a long way out and suddenly I found myself thinking about sharks. I don't think I've ever swum faster in my life than I did that night swimming back to shore. When I could touch bottom I ran out of the water and threw myself down on the beach, gasping, and when two guys ran up and asked me if I was all right I was still panting so hard I couldn't speak but could only nod. As the guys walked away I could hear them speculating about what drugs I had taken, but that night I had taken none at all.

There were some boyfriends during those years, although I often said I didn't want one, but they were not the men I saw in the gym or in the Pines; they were other, different men, and even today I do not understand why I found these men more attractive than all the beautiful men I was constantly surrounded with. Do not misunderstand me; these men—my boyfriends—were beautiful too. There was a Japanese dancer I met in the baths who broke all of the stereotypes of Oriental men: He was taller than I am, muscular, and aggressive, though he was very kind too. There was a striking, dark-skinned black man with a physique that was totally flawless whom I met at the Saint one night, and we danced together and had sex together for a few months before drifting apart. There was a young Mexican boy (he told me he was eighteen but I didn't believe him) who saw me in a restaurant where he bused tables and followed me home. He spoke almost no English and I spoke no Spanish, so our communication was mostly physical. There were some others too, mostly black men who did fit the well-known stereotype, but I loved no one. No, I loved life, sex, beauty, freedom, and I thought it all would never end.

In those days young men did not think about death. True, the gay press was beginning to heat up its coverage of AIDS, periodically unleashing hysterical, incomprehensible outbursts, but I ignored it, as did most of my friends, and then two things happened. In the spring my grandfather died suddenly of a heart attack, and I remember standing looking at his gray, waxy face in the casket, imagining what he would say about the fact that there was makeup on it, being sad that we had never again been friends after that fight we had in

Maine, and thinking for the first time how God damned awfully final death is. We all know intellectually that death is final and that it will get us someday just like it has everyone else through the ages, but that afternoon when I looked at Grandfather's face was the first time I realized, I *knew*, that someday I would end up just like that. In the weeks and months following Grandfather's funeral I began to read all of the news about AIDS that I could find, and I began to change my life. I didn't yet begin to practice what is now called "safe sex," but I did dramatically reduce the number of men I had sex with. It was not easy. I only went to the baths once or twice a month, and when I went I only had sex with one man, and sometimes I did not have sex at all. On one of the visits to the baths during that period after I had sex with a man I realized I knew him somehow, and he said he thought he knew me too. It took us a good half hour of jointly searching our memories to figure out that he was Alex, whose name I had by then forgotten, the guy Teddy had seen me kissing the evening of the fight that had broken us up two years earlier. Alex and I exchanged little pieces of paper with our phone numbers on them, as people often did at the baths, and although I didn't expect to hear from him he did call, and we have become friends. I introduced him to Teddy when we were back together again, and at first I thought Teddy was going to cause a scene as he used to do in the War Years, but Alex is a playwright and he got Teddy talking about the theater and the bad moment passed. They became good friends, and often when I came home from work I would find them discussing some play or other that I had never heard of. Alex still comes by at least once a week and calls often and it was his idea that I write all this down, but of course I'm getting things out of order again.

I didn't spend as much time in the Pines the summer after Grandfather died as I had in previous years, and it wasn't because of AIDS either. I was working hard on Wall Street and traveling frequently on business, and often when Friday evening came I just wanted to stay in the city and relax. When I did go to the Island everyone always talked about AIDS—the latest new disease (before then most people seemed to have KS—The Cancer, as it was called), the latest death, the latest crank treatment—and it seemed that everyone but me had a close friend who had died from it. However, that changed. I can remember so well that clear, beautiful fall day when Wayne called and told me that Sean, my friend from the gym, had it and was moving back to Seattle to be close to his family. Sean and I had become for a while, in 1981 and '82, what is called in the gay world "gym buddies," working out together and then afterward sometimes going for a beer or two or something to eat, but then my schedule became unpredictable and we gradually stopped going to the gym together and by the time I am telling about I had not seen him at all for six or nine months. I called him immediately after Wayne hung up and asked if I could come to see him that night, and I was there within an hour. He looked fine to me and I told him so and then without speaking he pulled off his shirt and pushed his pants down to his knees and showed me the dark purple marks on his still-beautiful body. I gasped and shut my eyes and I did not know what to tell him: What do you tell a beautiful young man who thinks life is the proverbial banquet with no end in sight and who finds out he has been condemned to death? Even now I cannot answer that question.

I saw Sean only once more before he left, and that fall, for the first time in my life, I was badly depressed; all I could think about was ending up like Sean and then like my grandfather. Although I am no longer depressed about this damned disease—if anything I am angry—my depression then was a hard, determined one that I could not break out of, and I began to come home after work and drink and take cocaine and I would do this for two or three weeks until I could stand it no longer and then rush off to the bars or baths and have sex while thinking, is this the man who is going to kill me? My depression was at its worst at Christmas that year, when I refused to go to Maine and instead spent several days before Christmas alone in my apartment without going out at all. Christmas morning someone knocked on the door and I remember that I wasn't going to answer it, but whoever it was was very persistent and I finally opened the door in anger to find John and Patty, from the next apartment, with a gift for me. They could see inside the apartment, and they could see that I had no Christmas tree or decorations (I had always decorated the apartment in the past), and when they asked about it I said that I wasn't in any mood for Christmas, and then John told me he was kidnapping me. I finally did agree to have Christmas dinner with them and their other guests, and I got very drunk and I began to talk about Ted and about AIDS. I guess I was not behaving very well because quite early in the evening John said that he was taking me home, and he did and he came in with me and I talked to him for hours. The next morning I couldn't remember the conversation and I called John to apologize, and he asked me over for dinner again that night. Since then we have become very close friends, and he is *straight*! As Teddy said to me last year, after John kissed me good-bye at the door, "Dear, he's a *breeder*. You *must* be slipping."

My depression held on through the winter, although it was not a steady pressure but came in waves and then left me exhausted and with a bad feeling in my head. By that time the Saint was no longer the newest, hottest club—it was no longer the place where everyone from the A-list could be found on Saturday nights—but I began to go there more frequently than I had since the season it opened. Most of my friends only went there on Big Party nights, so it was a place where I could be with beautiful men and yet be alone, standing on the outside of the dance floor and watching or sometimes dancing with strangers but usually slipping away if I saw someone I knew. I remember one night when a beautiful dark-haired boy with blue eyes and perfect teeth stood beside me at the bar while we waited for sodas and suddenly looked at me and smiled and asked me if I wanted to dance. I said no, I didn't dance much anymore, and he took my arm and pulled me away from the bar and said that this time I was dancing whether I wanted to or not, and I laughed and agreed. We danced for a while—he told me he was nineteen—and then I offered him cocaine. We went to the balcony to do it, and after we each took some he offered me a bottle of poppers, which I accepted, and then when I was still feeling the rush from the poppers he knelt down and unzipped my pants, and for a few minutes it felt so good and I looked through the dimly transparent dome at the flashing lights and heard the music and put my hands on the back of his head and began to move my hips and then suddenly, clearly, I thought, my God, I could be killing this young man, cutting off his life, destroying that beauty, and I pushed him away so hard he fell on his back, and before he could get up I ran down the tight-curving metal stairs, doing up my pants as I ran, and then ran out the door without even stopping at my locker to get my coat. Poor Wayne was coming in as I was leaving, and he grabbed me to give me a hug. I shouted, "Get out of my way!" and pushed him aside and ran down the street. I ran until I was hot, perspiring, panting, trying to run from the death I was sure was within me.

I began to feel better with the coming of spring. Sex still frightened me, but I had begun to use condoms and to insist that my partners use them also, and somehow as the air became warmer and the days lengthened and I could again hear the doves and sparrows outside my bedroom window and see the forsythia in golden bloom in the courtyard my six-month-long depression broke up and became only an unpleasant memory, although sometimes it would suddenly unexpectedly return for an hour or two and then leave just as suddenly. Around me people died of AIDS, but I saw it as if from a distance; it no longer moved me. I took my usual share in the Pines that summer, and I found the Island only a grim shadow of what it had been and what I had loved. (Interestingly enough, the following summer when Teddy and I were together again the Pines seemed to have regained some of its former life: There were fewer vacant houses; beautiful men again roamed the beach and talked to strangers; at parties people talked about something other than AIDS.) As I think about that year now, it seems as though I were living in a dream. I even remember it in slow motion: being cruised in a crowded subway car that crawled along the tracks; coming out of work in the evenings and walking as though I were suspended in some clear, viscous fluid; braving the sun as it hung in the sky for hours without moving.

Winter came again, hard, cold, and unpleasant, when

I could no longer enjoy even the sight of pretty young men with bare arms or chests or legs, when the days grew shorter and the social season swelled. I went to concerts, plays, films, brunches, museums; I skated; I spent many hours in the gym, working harder than ever before; I swam; I did not play the piano. I enjoyed my life. I was, I was told, and I thought it too, "hot"; I was successful; I was well educated; and I was completely unobtainable, resisting all attempts to marry me off to someone like myself, or to anyone. I was always invited to parties, to dinners, to brunches, as the Eligible Man; I was introduced to doctors, lawyers, other investment bankers. I remember one party shortly before Christmas that year when I found the company so perfect, so smug, so *intolerable,* that I spent the evening in the kitchen joking with the waiter. My host, a lawyer who lived in a lawyer-only house in the Pines in the summers and gave professional-only parties, pulled me into one of the bedrooms and told me that I was behaving badly and that the waiter was nothing but a hustler. I smiled and thanked the man for his advice and then went into the kitchen, took off my jacket, rolled up my sleeves, and helped clean up. I took the waiter home with me and we got high on cocaine and made love, safely, and it was the first time I had made love, which is different than having sex, in a long time. I remember I asked the guy afterward if he was a hustler, and he said, "Sometimes. But this isn't one of them," and he said if anything he should pay me, and I laughed. The next morning I called the man who had given the party and thanked him, and he was very rude. We have not spoken since.

I had assumed that the family would not be going to Maine that Christmas because Grandfather had died and Grandmother's arthritis was making it painful for her to walk or to ride in a car for long periods of time, but Grandmother insisted on going, saying that she wanted to see Maine in the winter just one more time, so we all went. (As I write this Grandmother is still quite healthy and it is I who will probably not see Maine in the winter again.) My family wanted me to ride up with them, but I said I preferred to drive by myself and also that if I went up in my own car I could go a day or two earlier and get the house ready. The day I drove up was clear and very cold, but it did not snow (as I got farther north there was snow on the ground, of course) and as I drove I found myself thinking fondly and sadly about Teddy, as I guess all people, gay or straight, do about their first lost love, and those two nights I was in the house alone I saw him— us—everywhere, making love in front of the windows that faced the sea, sleeping on the rug in front of the fire, cooking together in the kitchen, walking through the snow. I missed him more than I ever had since we broke up, and I remember that the evening the family arrived Dad said he wished Ted were there and Mother gave him a hard look that said very clearly, "shut up," and I said it was okay, I missed him too. It was the first time we'd talked about him and we all reminisced a little, carefully avoiding mentioning the scene with Grandfather; even Grandmother said that Ted had been a nice young man, for an actor.

We made it through the Christmas festivities, which were smaller and more subdued than they had been in earlier years because many of the Young Ones had moved away or now had families of their own and several members of Grandfather's generation had died, and Christmas night I again went to the Pine Tavern. It was terrible; before it had had a beauty and classiness of its own, but it had been sold and renovated to become a tawdry imitation of the discos I had left behind in New York. Not much of the old crowd was there, and the ones who were introduced wives and passed around photographs of smiling babies and well-scrubbed children. Everyone knew I was gay, either having been there when I was there with Teddy or having heard about it, but no one said anything about it until I was ready to leave, when someone asked me about Ted and told me that a boyhood friend from the town, the guy who had squeezed my leg the night I said Teddy was my lover, had died of AIDS. It started to snow while I drove back to the house, and the snow made me think of Ted even more and I began to worry.

When I returned to New York I called Wayne and asked him if he had heard from Ted, and he said no, not for a couple of years, and after I spoke to Wayne I called everyone I could think of who might have his address, but no one did. I continued to think about him occasionally, but it was a busy spring and I abandoned my search and then, the first time I was on the Island, in mid-April, someone said he thought he had seen him in New York. I had never been on the Island so early in the season before, but Wayne had bought a house, most of which he was renting to his old friends to help pay the mortgage, and he decided to have a party to celebrate the closing. It was a great idea, actually; everyone who came out for the weekend had to stop by Wayne's apartment in the city and pick up something and bring it out with them, and I drove a carload of stuff myself. It was a cold, rainy, wet weekend, but one filled with good feelings, and as we sat around the fire one night while rain tore at the house someone said that he thought he had seen Teddy in New York, but he had been in a cab and the man he thought was Teddy was walking on the sidewalk and he wasn't sure, and once again I missed him.

I can remember the next week as if it were last week. The storm drifted out to sea and pulled warm, sweet air up from the south in its wake. I went to work without a topcoat and on that Wednesday, when I was out of the office at lunch hour, I saw a beautiful young man, probably a messenger or clerk, lying back on a bench with his shirt off and his arms spread wide, and I wanted him. I didn't proposition him, of course, but instead went to a bathhouse in the area that was filled at lunchtime with men from Wall Street, a place where a partner in a firm could have sex with a boy from the mailroom of the same firm and they both would be happy. I met someone there that day and we had very safe sex (we masturbated together), and then the guy asked me for a date and when I offered my phone number and told him to call me he said no, let's fix a date now. It was not something I usually did, but it was a beautiful day and I was in a good mood so I said yes, and we agreed to meet for drinks at the Plaza on Saturday. When Saturday came I had decided not to go (the thought of which makes me shake now) but then, fifteen minutes before I was supposed to be there, I changed my mind and dressed quickly in a blue blazer and chinos and caught a cab and was running up the steps of the Plaza when I bumped into him, my Teddy, and I didn't recognize him and he called to me and I stopped and turned and when I saw him I thought, and I remember this so clearly, please God, not him, and I did not know what to say.

Chapter 7

It was the kind of spring day you think about on a miserable winter's day that is bleak and cold, when it is dark at five o'clock and you are rushing home, face chapped by the wind, fingers so cold they hurt, feet wet, and you think, I wish it were spring, and you imagine a day when the sky holds only a few high-moving clouds, the sun is warm but not hot, the air comfortable, refreshing, a day too warm for a jacket but too cool for short sleeves, a day when the birds all sing, a day when you can smell flowers. It was that kind of day. I remember my first thoughts as if they were a distinct, slow sequence, although they probably took less than a second. First his appearance registered—my Teddy, who had once been so healthy, so beautiful, so physical, was thin and had the face of someone much older than he was, with dark circles, almost like bruises, under his eyes; then I thought, he has AIDS; then an involuntary prayer came—Please God, oh *please* not Teddy; then there was a tiny flash of optimism and I can remember thinking maybe he doesn't have it but that flash was quickly extinguished by the certainty that he did. I didn't know what to say and I couldn't make my voice work just to say hello and I knew that Teddy knew what I was thinking and then he took my hand and shook it and held it a second with his other hand on top of it and said, "You look great." I was aware that we were blocking the steps—that people were trying to get around us—and that a limousine was unloading at the curb, but it was like a dream. I remember wondering how they kept the green carpeting on the steps so clean, and I remember I finally said, "Are you all right?" Ted tried to laugh and said, "I just lost some weight," and when he said that I put my hands on his shoulders and held him at arm's length to look at him, and beneath my hands there were no longer those beautiful layers and ridges of muscle; he was so thin I could feel the bones, which seemed to be barely covered with flesh. His face was browner than his neck and the top of his chest, and I realized that he was wearing makeup. I rubbed a finger on his cheek and then held it out to him, clearly smudged brown, and his eyes met mine and he turned away. I don't know why, but I exploded into a quick rage and yelled, "Where the fuck do you think you're going!" People stopped to watch, amused I'm sure by what they thought to be a little spat between two homosexuals, and that made me even madder, and then Teddy said, "Leave me alone," and tried to pull his arm away again. I don't know why I was so angry, but I was, and I squeezed his arm so hard I could see in his face that it hurt, and when I saw that my anger dissolved as quickly as it had come and I told him I just wanted to talk to him, and then that son of a bitch said, "I don't want your pity."

I remember that I said to Teddy, "We're going to talk," and I held his arm, although not so tightly, and walked him down Central Park South. It was, as I have said, a beautiful spring day when people carried their jackets and the forsythia in bloom spread a yellow haze across Central Park. I didn't know where I was taking him, but when I saw that the cafe at the St. Moritz was open I told him we were having lunch and he said nothing. While we waited for the maitre d' Teddy was quiet and I held his arm so he would not run away, and when we got a table we sat in silence for a few minutes and looked at the menu and then Teddy put his down and said that he didn't want anything, although he had read the menu carefully, and I was sure it was because he could not afford it so I ordered for both of us and then rested my elbows on the table and my chin on my hands and said, "Talk to me." Teddy didn't say anything at first but looked away at a carriage across the street, and then he said, "How's the piano coming?" The next ninety minutes were like that. He wouldn't answer a direct question; instead, he'd respond with a non sequitur or with another question or he'd just gaze out at the park, although occasionally he'd let down his guard a little and say, "It's so good to see you." He looked so tired, and once he started to cry, and I remember I finally told him that I wasn't leaving his side until he told me the whole story. He was silent for a few minutes, and then it all spilled out in a rush; he'd had KS for almost two years and then, a couple of months before we were speaking, a bout of PCP. I put my hand on top of his when he told me, and he looked into my face then put his head down on his arms on the table and sobbed, making a sucking sound as he tried to stop himself; I cried too then, a strange kind of crying that didn't affect my breathing but where tears ran freely from my eyes and down my face. I guess we were attracting a lot of attention, because a waitress came over and asked loudly, insultingly, if everything was *all right,* and I told her, very plainly, "Fuck off," and Teddy, still sobbing on his arms, said through his gasps, "Yeah!" I know it wasn't an appropriate time for laughter, but that "Yeah" showed me that Teddy was still Teddy, and I giggled, and Teddy lifted his head and looked at me and smiled a little, and I know this was terrible, but the sight of him smiling at me with his makeup streaked and running made me laugh aloud, and I said, "Dear, you *must* fix your face," and then he laughed too.

It took about a half hour for us to argue again. Teddy did retire, to the men's room I hope, to fix his makeup and then we talked for a while about the War Years, although we did not yet call them that, and he laughed a little, and finally he said that he was tired and had to go, and I said I was going home with him. Well, Teddy told me I wasn't and I told him I was and he told me that I'd always been a stubborn bastard and I started to raise my voice in reply, but then I stopped and said quietly, "You bet." I paid the check and held his arm firmly as we left, and I hailed a cab at the curb. When we got in Teddy sat with his arms folded across his chest and wouldn't speak. "Where to?" the driver asked; "Where do you live?" I asked Teddy; "None of your business," Teddy told me. Then the driver told us to either decide or get out so I told him to drive around the outside of Central Park and I told Teddy I thought I had enough money to do it for about six hours and after then I'd have to stop at a bank. We made one round in silence, up Central Park West, across 110th Street, and down Fifth Avenue. I looked out the window, watching people—I remember leaning forward to watch a beautiful black man on roller skates crossing in front of us when we were stopped for a light—and Teddy looked at his lap. When we reached our starting point the driver stopped and said, "Well?", and I told him to do it again. He was not pleased and he started up with a lurch that threw us back against the seat and he mumbled, I think, "God damned faggots." I couldn't hear exactly what he said and when I could sit up I asked him if he'd kindly repeat it. He wouldn't, and we had a wild ride up Central Park West; he'd accelerate toward yellow lights and then if one turned red before he got there he'd come to a screeching, jarring stop. After that happened two or three times Teddy yelled, "All right!" and leaned forward and gave the driver the address. Teddy did not look at me and we did not speak until we reached the place, and then after I'd paid the driver Teddy said to him, "Ass*hole*!"

I didn't like the looks of Teddy's building at all. Two drunken men lying on the steps drinking from quart bottles of beer asked us for money when we went inside; a man was sleeping on the floor huddled against a wall in the lobby, which smelled like marijuana and stale beer; the elevator smelled like feces. "So what were you doing in the Plaza?" I asked as we rode up to his floor. "None of your fucking business," he said. "You know," I said, "you really are a dickhead sometimes." "I thought you liked dickheads," he said, and then, as the elevator door opened, "I was taking a piss." The hall to his room smelled like urine, sweat, and cigarettes; the walls were filthy; there was a cigarette burn-scarred carpet on the floor that probably had once been orange but was now dark brown. "Christ," I said. Teddy unlocked his door and held it open for me and he seemed like a broken man, ashamed but no longer caring. There was a bed, a small, old dresser that had once been painted white but was now gray and marked, a bar with some clothes hanging from it, and one wooden chair; there was an uncovered light fixture that held two bulbs, and there was a window, dark with grime, that looked out on a black air shaft. "Christ!" I said again. While I looked out the window Teddy sat on the bed with his hands on his face and his elbows on his knees, and I wanted to hold him so much, but I knew it wasn't the time to do it so I asked where the bathroom was and he told me that it was at the end of the hall and that I'd need the key hanging by his door. I won't describe the bathroom except to say that the Mine Shaft after a long weekend night was probably cleaner. Of course, we fought when I got back to his room. I told him he was going home with me and he said he wasn't and called me a nasty name or two, so I looked around until I found a duffel bag and a suitcase under the bed and started packing his things. He still had the sweaters Mother and I had given him for Christmas, and when I found them, well worn but neatly folded in his drawer, I almost cried. He also had the leather jacket he was wearing the night we met, and when I started to pack that he said no, he'd carry it, and then I knew he was coming. As I think about it now I think he probably wouldn't have agreed so easily if he had not been so tired, but poor Teddy was exhausted. He fell asleep in the cab on the way back to my apartment.

The next couple of months were very difficult for both of us. Teddy was determined he wasn't going to depend on me and often he treated me quite meanly. It was as if he was there against his will but was too tired to fight hard enough to cause us to separate again, although we certainly did fight, not the monumental battles of the War Years but little skirmishes that were never completely resolved and left us both angry. We even argued again the first night he was back. He said he wouldn't sleep in the bed with me because he looked too bad and he also didn't want me to be exposed to him; I said that if anyone slept on the couch it would be me; he wanted pajamas so I wouldn't see his lesions; I told him he was being stupid; he called me names. I finally found a pair of loose beach pants and a T-shirt for him and he changed in the bathroom. By this time I was very angry, but I didn't know how to treat him because of his illness so I seethed but didn't do much until he actually started to make a bed for himself on the couch, and then I told him, very quietly, that if he didn't get into bed I'd put him there, and I took off my shirt so he could see my muscles. He wouldn't admit it, of course, but I could tell that he was impressed, and he went into the bedroom and got into bed, hugging the edge and making his body take as little space as possible. That night, for the first time in years, I slept in my underwear.

I didn't go to work the next day, and Teddy slept late, gathering energy for what was to be another fight that evening. When he finally got up I made him some breakfast and spent a long time just getting necessary information from him—he had almost no money and no job (he was in the process of being evicted from the room I had seen) but he did have Medicaid—and then I went out to shop. The poor dear wanted pajamas, so I thought I'd do a nice thing and I went to Sulka and got him a pair of beautiful gray silk ones. I waited until bedtime to give them to him and as soon as he saw the name on the box he started screaming at me, saying he didn't want charity and he didn't want pity and that he was going to find someplace else to live, and then when he opened the box he screamed that he didn't want three-hundred-dollar pajamas and he locked himself in the bathroom and cried for half an hour. I remember being mad as hell at him but thinking that I couldn't do anything about it because he had AIDS.

We continued to argue over the next couple of months until finally he pushed me too far and I hit him. It seemed as though we fought about everything; it seemed as though he *wanted* to fight, and I think now that it was probably a way for him to show that he was alive, a way for him to seize a place in my life when I had everything he didn't: health; vitality; friends; money. He wouldn't see any of his old friends for those first months, not even John and Patty from next door, and not only would he not *see* any of his old friends (I could understand him being sensitive about his appearance), he wouldn't even speak to them on the telephone. I called Wayne the day after Teddy came back and asked him to come over for dinner the day after that, and when I told Teddy he said that if Wayne came for dinner he would move out, and I think he meant it. When I saw Wayne at the gym that night I told him about this, and he called Teddy on the telephone and when Teddy said hello and Wayne started to talk, Teddy hung up. After then Teddy wouldn't answer the telephone at all, and I couldn't get him to agree to see or speak to anyone. I remember I finally said he was acting like a child, and his response was, "So, I'll move out." We fought about money, too. He had very little and at first he would do nothing to get the disability benefits he was entitled to. That was all right with me because I had enough money to support both of us, but he wouldn't take any of that either. He wouldn't let me buy him anything except food, but if I offered him cash so he could buy things for himself he screamed at me. Finally, to make sure that he had access to money if he needed it or wanted it in a hurry I left five hundred dollars in a box in the top drawer of my dresser and told him he could take what he wanted from it without telling me in advance and that I would periodically replenish it. Of course, he wouldn't touch a dime, but at least I tried.

The main problem between us those first months, however, was not money or his antisocial behavior, it was Fire Island, although one of the problems about Fire Island was that he didn't want to see any of his old friends. I had again rented a room in Wayne's house, and I was looking forward to going out because, although a few people in the house changed every year, there was still a group of us who had known each other since that first summer Teddy took me there and we were closer than family; no, we *were*, and *are*, family. Teddy would not go—he would not even talk about it— so I decided that I would spend the weekends in the city with him instead of going to the Island, and of course we argued about it. Everyone in the Island house was getting together for the first time the third weekend in May and when I asked Teddy to go out with me he said, "No," and nothing else, but then when I told him I'd stay home too he screamed at me to leave him alone and said that he didn't need pity. I didn't go, and the next two or three weeks were tense; we barely spoke to each other and tried to avoid each other in the apartment. I hadn't mentioned the Island in a couple of weeks, but then one lovely evening early in June I brought the subject up again. It was a clear day that faded into a deep crystal-blue Maxfield Parrish dusk, and we sat together looking out over the city as the sky dimmed and lights came on, remembering a similar evening almost exactly six years earlier when Teddy and I had first moved into his apartment and had drunk Champagne and eaten dinner by candlelight and then later spent hours holding and cuddling and making love. As we sat here last year, in the very place I am writing this, neither of us mentioned that earlier evening, but I knew Teddy was remembering it as well as I, and while I was making dinner—chicken breasts cooked with Sauternes and leeks—Teddy asked if we could have candles. We ate dinner by candlelight and almost totally in silence and when we were through, although I knew Teddy drank almost nothing anymore, I got a bottle of Champagne from the refrigerator and two glasses and poured Champagne for us both and, as we sat and looked out over the City of Magic, I said, "Remember?" and Teddy nodded, yes.

Exactly how we got from that quiet, gentle time to a screaming fight I'm not sure, but I remember when we were ready for bed—I in my underwear, Teddy in beach pants and T-shirt—I decided that I wanted more Champagne, although I had drunk most of the first bottle, so I opened another bottle and brought it and two clean glasses to bed with me and Teddy and I sat up against the headboard with glasses in our hands and looked out at the night sky. I started talking about the first summer we had gone to the Island together (we laughed about the feather party), and then I asked, a little belligerently I admit, why he wouldn't go with me again, and I talked about all the things I had done on the Island in the years we were apart, and suddenly he interrupted me by saying, "So go! Just shut up and go! You just go out there and find someone else! You won't have any trouble; you're still a pretty boy!" Before then I almost had begun to think that he didn't care for me anymore but was just staying with me because it was convenient, but when I heard that old jealousy I knew he still cared for me at least a little, and I started to reassure him when he exploded with, "I can't do it now, but boy, I used to be able to!" and he told me, in great detail, about some of the men he had secretly had sex with during the years we lived together, and then I was enraged. At some point he said, "Boy, were you ever stupid," and I slapped his face so hard it had a hand print on it that lasted for a day.

I gasped as soon as I did it, shocked that I had hit someone with AIDS, and at the same instant Teddy looked at me, equally shocked, and I started to say that I was sorry but he put his finger over my lips so I wouldn't say it and we were silent. There was a lot of understanding in the silence, and after a minute or two he put his arms up, indicating a hug but not sure if it was all right to grab me, and I pulled him down and we held each other tightly, and for the first time it was he who was the weaker and thinner of the two of us. After a while we sat up again, and as we did I said, "I thought it was back to the war years," and Teddy laughed and said that was what they had been all right, and from that time we called them that: the War Years.

We talked for hours that night and we finally reached an understanding: He had AIDS and he *was* going to accept my help; he *was* going to go to the Island; I was *not* going to see any other men; if he wore pajamas he was damned well going to wear the ones I had bought him.

It was a great night. Sometime around two in the morning he asked me to play the piano for him. I hadn't played at all in months and hadn't practiced in years, and I said I couldn't play, but of course Teddy insisted so then I said, "What about the neighbors?" and Teddy said, "Fuck the neighbors!" so I played a little nocturne that Teddy said was boring and he said didn't I know anything a little livelier and I laughed and although I had not played the piece in years I rattled off a very, very bad, very, very loud performance of Prokofiev's *Toccata*. The phone rang in the middle of it and Teddy answered it while I still played. It was John, next door, calling to ask if I would please stop and Teddy, who had refused to see or talk to John for the previous two months said, when he heard who it was, "Hi, dear, it's Ted. Are you *still* straight?" John said he was coming over, and Teddy changed into those new pajamas in seconds. It was, as I said, a great night. When John came in it was obvious that Teddy didn't want to touch him first and there was a second or two of awkward silence and then John said, "Come here, you son of a bitch," and there was a big hugging session. We all talked and after a half hour or so Teddy excused himself, saying he was tired, but John and I stayed up and talked until the sky was light and the birds were calling in the courtyard. Neither of us made it to work.

Teddy was up before I was the next morning and when I got up, around noon, he made breakfast for us, and then after breakfast he said he was going to buy some "decent beer." "Bitch, bitch, bitch," I said, and he said, "You never did have any taste." When he was gone I called Dad first, and then Mother (I had told them earlier that Teddy was back but not that he was ill), and I had long conversations with both of them, telling them that I intended to stay with Teddy until the end. They were both really wonderful, saying that they wanted to see him again and that they would help in any way they could, including financially. I remember thinking after I talked to them what a lucky man I was to have the parents I did, but as I have come to know more people with this damned disease I have found that in most cases their families are wonderful too: Mothers, fathers, brothers, sisters, and in-laws, and even ex-wives, have all taken this disease as a personal enemy and have done everything they could to help those they love fight it, and I know it would be a lot harder for many of us without their help. But I've gotten off the track again (I remember that in college one of my professors used to lecture me again and again for not taking one idea and following it through). Teddy came back early that afternoon with two six-packs of St. Pauli Girl, and when he put it away he left two bottles out on the counter and asked me if I wanted one. I really didn't, I remember, but it seemed that he wanted me to have one so I said yes and he opened the beers and handed one to me and sat down.

I remember that afternoon too well. He sat beside me at the table and we looked out at the courtyard, silent for a moment, and then he said, "I'm going to die, you know, and we've got to talk about it." I said what I thought were all the right things, that he wasn't necessarily going to die, that if he was it would be a long time in the future, and that in any case he was still living and should concentrate on that, but Teddy, and he was right, would not be put off. He said, "No, we're going to talk about it *now*," and we did. He told me what he expected was going to happen to him physically—it turned out that he was almost right—and he told me that he wanted no attempts made to revive him once he started to die. He was very insistent on the last point; I remember him saying, "You promise, no heroic efforts. I want to die with dignity," and I promised, and I told him to write something about what he wanted and sign it and have it notarized. But he wasn't finished; he wanted to talk about what I was to do *after* he died, which I didn't want to talk about at all. He wanted no funeral, no service, no nothing; he wanted to be cremated and he didn't want me or anyone else to claim the ashes but wanted the undertaker (what a horrible word) to dispose of them. He said all this with great braveness, very firmly and deliberately, and when he was finished I got another beer for myself (he had only taken a few sips of his), but then when I got back to the table he said, "Andy, I can't take the needles," and his voice almost broke. I didn't know anything then, so I said, "They don't hurt," and he looked at me sadly and said, "I hope you never find out." We were quiet again—as Teddy grew closer to death we spent increasing amounts of time together in comfortable, contemplative silence—and Teddy said hesitantly, "There is one thing you could do." Of course I said, "Anything," and he asked me to memorize the 23rd Psalm and say it for him after he died. Unlike Teddy I had never been much for religion, but I agreed, thinking it was something he would forget. He didn't, of course; throughout the months he nagged me about it and quizzed me on it and coached me in how to recite it until, in the end, I came to love it as much as he did. I did recite it after he died, I recited it good, and I realized that Teddy's insistence about it was a way for him to feel like he was participating in his own death and even surviving beyond it, and it also helped to comfort me. However, I'll tell about that later.

Teddy was very tired after our conversation and said he needed a nap, and I remember I asked if it was all right to have Wayne over for dinner and Teddy said okay, but he seemed so scared, and so uncomfortable with the idea, that I almost changed my mind while he was sleeping. However, I finally decided it would probably be good for him to see Wayne, who had been a friend such a long time, so I called Wayne at work (he designs children's clothes) and when I asked him he said he was ready to leave immediately, but I told him to let Teddy rest. I went shopping, and when Teddy woke up I was in the kitchen doing obscene things to lobsters with the objective of ending up with an elegant-looking and hopefully good-tasting lobster and truffle salad. Teddy came to the kitchen door and looked and he said, "You're making a *mess!*" and he sat me down with another beer and started to work, and I experienced such a strong feeling of déjà vu I was dizzy. I could see us preparing the great meals that we had made together during the War Years, when Teddy had always accused me of being incompetent, and for a few minutes I was terribly sad, but it passed and I thought about the present and I was a little worried about how Teddy and Wayne would get along after all those years. My worry was needless. Wayne came in, handed me a bottle of wine, and grabbed Teddy and gave him a big hug and said, "So how are you, you old whore? You look like hell!", and it was the right thing to say; there was no awkwardness, no embarrassment. Teddy responded with, "Haven't you found a husband *yet!*" and then Wayne, the bastard, said, "Where are you putting your stereo this time?" It was a nice evening. My parents called and Teddy talked to them on the phone in the bedroom; he agreed to go to the Island; Wayne said he would get Teddy some better makeup; Teddy made me clean up, saying that after all he was the one who was sick, and besides he'd had to dismember the lobsters. We made love that night, and it was really really nice to have my Teddy in my arms again. We played very safely, of course (over the next few months we elevated the Princeton Rub to the artistic level of Kabuki theater), but it didn't make any difference; it was as if the years apart had never happened, as if AIDS didn't exist.

We settled into a quiet life that included Teddy's illness but was not centered around it. We had to make allowances for time for doctor's visits and afternoon naps, I took more time off from work than I should have, and when we went out, which was not often, we had to allow Teddy time to put on his makeup which, although he didn't look that bad without it, he insisted on wearing if he left the apartment, even to go downstairs to get the mail. In previous years I had usually planned to be out on the Island during the annual Gay Pride March on Fifth Avenue, but when I proposed that Teddy make his grand return to the Pines on Gay Pride Weekend he surprised me by firmly refusing, and we argued a little about it. I remember I told him that I enjoyed being gay and I enjoyed being with other gay men but that I did not enjoy spending a day with 100,000 of them and that although I was happy being gay I didn't think I was either proud or ashamed, I just *was* gay. Teddy pulled me to the windows that faced west and said, "Look, what do you see?" This apartment is on the back side of the sixth and top floor of its building and faces a courtyard that runs the entire length of the block between the buildings on this street and the buildings on the next one, and I looked and said I saw trees, a little pink in the sky over New Jersey, and the rogue parakeet that lived outside and was sitting on the fire escape of the next building trying to sound like a sparrow. "Look again," Teddy said, and he pointed. "In that apartment there with the lights two lovers are making dinner, next door two guys are cleaning their bedroom, that little garden down there was planted by two more lovers." As Teddy spoke two young men, one black, one white, climbed out of a window onto their fire escape and waved to Teddy and then sat with their arms around each other looking at the sunset. Teddy waved back; "See," he said, "that's what we're proud of; we're proud of the fact that we're able to tell the world to fuck off and just settle down and live our lives together, living—and dying—the way we choose, owning food processors and microwaves together and having sex from vanilla to S and M, or even dressing in pretty gowns if we want. That's what we're proud of, and one day a year we leave our microwaves and food processors and gay gyms and gay enclaves and come out and show the world just how proud we are." I thought about this a lot that night, and after Teddy went to sleep I typed what he had said and hung it on the refrigerator. Of course, he corrected it with a red pen the next morning, but I had gotten most of it, and he was right. We marched.

I called my friends the Pig Sisters, who are members of the New York City Gay Men's Chorus, the next morning and asked if we could march with them. In the past they had often asked me to spend Gay Pride Day with them, but I had always refused, preferring instead to go to a celebratory party or two in the Pines, and when I asked if we could march with them one of them asked me if I was feeling quite well, so I told them about Teddy. They had never met him, and Teddy was a little nervous the morning of the March, but when we all gathered on Central Park West they treated him as though they had known him all his life, each giving him a big kiss and then introducing him and me to everyone within grabbing distance. I thought it might be too much for Teddy, but it wasn't; he loved it. When the Chorus started moving the Sisters marched in the second row with Teddy between them and me on one side, and as we passed through Columbus Circle everyone joined hands and the Chorus sang "New York, New York" and received tremendous cheers. Teddy loved every minute of that day; he loved the crowds, the music, the good spirits. Sometimes he marched beside me and sometimes between the Sisters and sometimes he spent a few minutes beside some newfound friend that the Sisters introduced him to, and they *were* friends. When the Chorus reached St. Patrick's Cathedral it stopped and the huge crowd on the sidewalks became silent except for protesters in the next block who were holding a "prayer meeting" while holding signs telling us that we deserved to die. The Chorus stood in silence for a minute or two and then sang "Family" from *Dream Girls* and there were few dry eyes, and then after another minute or two of silence we started marching again while singing "Sometimes When We Touch," and I thought Teddy was going to break down completely because he did nothing to cover the tears running down his face. However, the Pig Sisters put us between them with their arms around us and we marched on, and we *were* a family.

There were many other emotional moments that day, but there were a lot of funny ones too. The Chorus was giving out recruitment flyers along the way, and whenever there was a particularly spectacular man someone would yell out, "Get him!" and someone would run out with a flyer and thrust it at the guy, and if he took it everyone in the Chorus would applaud. Somewhere in the thirties we spotted a young, very handsome policeman, which made one of the Sisters, who salivates when he sees a hot man in a uniform, weak in the knees, and I grabbed a flyer and rushed out and gave it to the policeman, who *took* it; when I got back in the ranks the Chorus sang "The Impossible Dream." Several times during the march friends of mine—often people with whom I'd had sex—ran out and gave me kisses, which finally made Teddy say, "It must have been a regular open house," which of course the Pig Sisters agreed with. But Teddy had some surprises too. Rollerina, who is a tall transvestite on roller skates who carries a star-tipped wand, whizzed *up* through the Chorus (we were marching downtown) dispensing magic and good cheer and when she saw Teddy she gave him a big hug before she whizzed on. People who don't know have wondered for years who Rollerina is in real life, and people who do know don't tell, and I said to Teddy, "You *know* her!" and Teddy just smiled and nodded, and the Chorus sang "New York, New York" again, and we walked on. When we reached Washington Square Teddy was exhausted and I wanted to take him home but he refused to go; no, he said very calmly that it would probably be his last March and he was going to finish it, and we did. As we walked toward the river the streets got narrower and the crowds grew and the men sang to unending cheers and applause and Teddy walked with his arm around me and around one of the Sisters and sang at the top of his voice (which wasn't very good), and he was right; I was proud to be gay and I was glad that I had marched, and this year, when I again marched with the Sisters, knowing then that I was ill, I could almost hear Teddy singing beside me and could almost feel his touch.

We went to the Pines on the following weekend, which was July Fourth. Teddy was very nervous and moving very slowly that Friday afternoon before we left, and I was trying to hurry him up because I'd told Wayne that we'd be there on a specific ferry. Teddy wouldn't be hurried, though; he laid out different combinations of clothes on the bed, going through practically everything we both owned to find things that looked, as he said, "sexy" but covered as much skin as possible, and then when he was packed he took a long time dressing. He wore the same loose white pants and white blousy shirt he had worn for the Gay Pride March, and when I saw his hands shake as he buttoned the shirt I pushed them away gently and buttoned it myself and kissed his nose. "Let's stay home," he said. "Nope," I told him, "You agreed. We're going." He was very quiet on the way out and in the ferry across the bay the person in the seat across from us stared hard at him and Teddy took my hand and held it very tightly. I was beginning to think myself that bringing him back to the Pines, where once he had been one of the hottest, most eligible men, was a bad idea, and what I was hoping would not happen at least until he'd been there a while and calmed down happened as soon as we got off the ferry. A guy Teddy had known before he knew me was standing on the dock waiting to meet someone and when he saw Teddy he said, "Ted!" and started to give him a hug and then stopped and said, "Oh my God," and Teddy took a big breath and said, "Ye-up, the Big A," and then the guy put his arms around Teddy and gave him a big hug and a big kiss. They talked for another minute or two and then the man the guy had been waiting for got off the ferry and the guy said he'd see Ted later and we started toward the house. I remember I said to Teddy, "See, that wasn't so bad," and Teddy said, "You remember him. You could park a Cadillac in that butt," and I pinched Teddy's nipple. Hard.

I knew there was going to be trouble as soon as we reached the walk to Wayne's house. There were three empty Champagne cases by the garbage pails and it sounded as though there was a party inside. Teddy said, "If that's a party I'm going home," and I remember thinking how nice it was that he called this apartment home but wondering what was going on in the house. I'm glad Wayne hadn't told me in advance or I would have kept Teddy in the city. We walked onto the deck into a crowd of thirty or forty people and Teddy said, "Oh. My. God.", and as soon as everyone saw Teddy they surrounded him and people kissed him and hugged him and everyone talked at once, and I was afraid that it might be too much for Teddy so I pushed my way to him and asked him if he was all right and, although there were tears in his eyes, he said he was fine, just fine. Wayne had invited as many of Teddy's old friends as he could find to a party for him, and what a party it was, not like those mass affairs on the Island where everyone drinks beer or some kind of red, alcoholic punch, but a party with Champagne and caviar and smoked salmon and lots of tiny hors d'oeuvres. Teddy was so happy and when I finally could get close to Wayne I remember I said, "You son of a bitch," and he said, "Well, it worked, didn't it?" It sure did work. Everyone drank Champagne and talked for an hour or perhaps an hour and a half, and then Wayne brought out a big cake that said "Welcome Back Ted" and everyone cheered.

My memories of that summer, the summer before last, are a montage of fragments stuck together in no particular chronological order, and when I think about that summer, as I am now, I find it strange that I can remember pieces of my youth and childhood better than I can remember it. I do remember a few things clearly, however. I remember walking to the store on the corner with Teddy one day and passing two beautiful men, obviously brothers, both probably in their mid-thirties, with dark hair, deep tans, and bright blue eyes, and Teddy saying, "God must have been smiling when he made those two," and then a week or two later seeing them walking on the beach in the Pines in the early evening, each holding the hand of another, equally beautiful man, and Teddy saying, "You know, it's sights like that that make me want to live as long as I can." I thought that was a little too serious for me, so I said, "I wonder if the brothers ever had sex together," and Teddy called me trash. I remember when Alex, the guy whom Teddy had seen me kissing the day we broke up, stopped by unexpectedly to return a book he'd had for six months, and I introduced him to Teddy, who was completely silent and wouldn't shake Alex's hand. I was sure he was going to start some kind of scene, but I told Alex, who is a playwright, that Teddy was an actor, and Alex asked Teddy what roles he had performed and the two of them talked for hours. After Alex left

Teddy said, "I want to know who fucked who." *"Whom,"* I said. "Whatever," Teddy said, although he knew English as well as I did, "I just want to hear the juicy details," and he called Alex "The Blond Boy with the Bubble Butt." The name Blond Boy stuck; I call him that now. From that night we began to think up nicknames for our friends. My cousin Daniel, who moved to New York that September, became "Dick of Death (or at least Large-Scale Destruction) Daniel"; Wayne became "Beautiful Bernice" because of his tendency to wear beautiful dresses, made by himself, at inappropriate occasions; John, whom Teddy constantly teased about being straight ("You know you really want it," Teddy'd say to him, and then he'd turn to me and say, "You know, he *needs* it."), received a nasty nickname that concerned the preferred site of his erotic life and which I will not tell here, and John's wife, Patty, became simply "Saint Patricia," because that's what she was; my mother became, to Teddy, "Mom," which I had never called her; and the Pig Sisters remained, as always, the Pig Sisters.

For most of that summer Teddy's health was stable, but toward the end of August he began to become very exhausted after even simple activities, and he began to have serious pains in his legs and knees and tremendous, incapacitating headaches that painkillers didn't touch. He never complained, but sometimes he would lay curled up in bed clenching his teeth so tightly the muscles in his face and neck showed clearly, and when this happened I would hold his hand and stroke his cheek and tell him not to fight the pain, to let it go, to let it wash over him like waves, and gradually he would relax and accept the pain without resistance and I would sit by him until he was asleep and then go into the bathroom and cry. Once he awoke and heard me and he came into the bathroom where I was sitting on the covered toilet crying and put his arms around my head and stroked it and held it tightly to his stomach and he, who was dying, comforted me.

We went to the Island a final time in the middle of September, going out on a Thursday and returning on Sunday. The first two days were perfect September days, warm but with cool, clear evenings, and we spent most of the time at home. Saturday, I remember, was cloudy, and Teddy said he wanted to go to Tea so we did. Everyone there was saying good-byes for the season, and Teddy spoke to everyone he knew, spending a few minutes in conversation and then moving on, sometimes with a kiss or a hug, and suddenly I realized that he was not just saying good-bye for the season, and I remember that as I watched him, so frail, I began for the first time to think clearly about his coming death. As darkness fell that evening thunder rolled in the south, out over the sea, and when Teddy was tired he put his arm around me and we left. We walked to the beach and down to the water without speaking, and while we stood there thunder continued to sound in the distance and lightning danced in the sky and flashed in broad sheets along the horizon. I remember Teddy turned to me and said, "God's talking," and I said to him, "If that's the case, I don't like what he's saying," and I said loudly, "If there is a God out there I defy him to put out his hand and save you!" and Teddy said to me, "But don't you see, it doesn't matter. This disease, it's part of life." "Why is it so much a part of *gay* life!" I cried, and Teddy held my hand and told me that it was important to remember that this damned disease is just a virus. It is not our *fault* that it infects us; it is just an organism that happens to flourish in the free-sex culture we developed. That does not mean that our culture was wrong; it only means that some insidious little organism has, in some kind of perverse Darwinist survival-of-the-fittest way, found us a physical medium in which to thrive.

We stayed on the beach until the rain started. Later, when the rain gusted hard across the Island, Teddy was in the worst pain I'd seen and he fought it hard, clenching his fists and stiffening his body when the pain hit him. Finally, however, he began to relax and breathe slow, deep breaths, and every breath brought with it a fresh, sharp wave that he allowed to wash over him without resistance.

Teddy lived about six months longer, and although he only died seven months ago I remember those final months, then days, hours, minutes, as though they were fragments of a distant dream that cannot be recalled in its entirety; only its emotional outlines and general contours still exist. Teddy was in a lot of pain, and I never left him alone except to go to work, and then when he became very ill I arranged shifts of friends to stay with him; Alex, Daniel, Wayne, John and Patty, and Mother all came and spent a morning or an afternoon, or sometimes the day, here while I worked. While he was still well enough to travel, however, he asked me if I'd give him the money to go to Hawaii to see his mother (his father, a serviceman, had died in Hawaii when Teddy was a child, and his mother had remained there), and of course I said that I was going with him and of course he said I wasn't, and, as always, we argued. I didn't go. I took him to the airport in a limousine and as I watched him walk slowly, almost shuffling, down the corridor beyond where I could not pass, I wondered if I would ever see him again.

Throughout the previous summer Teddy had often asked me to play the piano for him, and gradually I had started playing again, mostly loud, fast pieces that Teddy had liked, and during the two weeks he was away I practiced harder than I had for years and whipped my two old war-horses, Rachmaninoff's Second Sonata and Schumann's *Symphonic Etudes*, into playable condition. I remember that I spent a lot of time thinking about Teddy and missing him, and when I missed him I would play the *Goldberg Variations*, and now I cannot play the *Variations* without thinking about Teddy and then before him to when I was young.

I had intended to play one of my newly relearned

war-horses for Teddy when he came back, but when he
got off the plane he had a high fever and was soaked
with sweat and I took him directly to the hospital from
the airport. I was so mad at that damned hospital; even
with orders from his doctor it took a couple of hours to
get Teddy admitted and find a room for him, and he
was so sick. When he finally was given a bed he was
shaking so badly that he couldn't manage the buttons
on his shirt so, even though the nurse asked me to
leave, I undressed him myself and put him into one of
those absurd hospital gowns and into bed. Then an in-
tern came to start an IV and told me I had to wait
outside, and poor Teddy said, "Don't go," and held my
arm so tightly he bruised it. However, the doctor insisted so I went out into the hall and shut the door and
leaned against the wall beside it and when Teddy
screamed with pain I shut my eyes tightly and clenched
my fists. The doctor was in Teddy's room a long time
and when he finally left and I went back in Teddy was
so weak he could barely talk, and I held his hand and
wiped the sweat from his face. As I was doing that a
nurse came in and told me that I had to leave and I
started to argue, but Teddy squeezed my hand a little
and told me it was all right, and I left. I went to a bar
on the corner and drank so much I vomited on the sidewalk on the way home.

Teddy was in the hospital about three weeks with
PCP, and during that time I did not go to work but
spent an hour or two around lunch and dinnertime with

Teddy, bringing him food from outside (having been in the hospital for three weeks not long ago myself, I can truly report that hospital food is grim, grim, grim), and the rest of the time I spent at home playing the piano. After a few days on medication Teddy improved dramatically, and when I wasn't there he would put his IV bottle on a pole with wheels and visit the other AIDS patients. After a few days of this one of the hospital's social workers started asking him if he'd mind visiting some patient who was either particularly depressed or who had had no visitors, and Teddy would always agree. I bought him a Sulka robe, gold and black, which he wore with the gray pajamas because, as he said, it is always all right to be fashionable, and often when I arrived at the hospital he was standing at the nurses' station, in his robe and pajamas, with a flower pinned to his lapel, gossiping with the nurses. The nurses genuinely seemed to like him, and the staff treated him all right, but after my own experiences I think that was probably because I was there so much. One morning a few days before he was discharged, however, I did get into a good argument with an aide. I went into Teddy's room and was stunned to see blood everywhere, on the bed, on the floor, in the sink, and no Teddy, and for a moment I thought the worst. Then an aide came in with clean sheets and told me that Teddy had had a problem with his IV and that he was in the shower down the hall cleaning up, and the aide dumped the sheets on the bed and *left*. I followed her down the hall (much as Mother did to a nurse a few months ago) screaming at her to come back and fix the room, but she just shook her head and walked on. I cleaned the room myself, and when Teddy came back everything was in order. He never knew that I had done it.

When Teddy was released from the hospital he was a different man. Before then, even though he was ill, there was something about him that was alive and vital, and after he came home from the hospital it was, for the most part, gone, replaced with a resignation to the inevitable, although with that resignation, that acceptance, there was a dogged, stubborn courage. He was never free from pain, but he never complained or even mentioned it unless I asked. Sometimes, when I knew the pain was severe, I *would* ask, although I already knew, saying "How is it?" and then sometimes he would say, "It's bad," and I would hold his hand and stroke his cheek and help him move from letting the crests of the waves of pain hurt him to just letting his entire body and mind flow with the waves themselves. Sometimes when I looked at him I could not help myself from thinking of an animal, a dog perhaps, that has been hit by a car and is lying, dying, by the side of the road and yet looks up at you trustingly with open eyes, as if to tell you, I'd really like to run and play I just can't right now.

Teddy talked a lot about dying too, but not so much about himself as about me. He said he was sad because

I would be living and grieving when he was at peace, and he encouraged me to look for a new boyfriend immediately after he died. "But not before!" he'd say, shaking a finger at me. We joked about that sometimes. Teddy would cut pictures of models—male, of course—from magazines and tape them on the refrigerator and consider them for a few days before deciding they were deficient in some way and replacing them with others. I remember one day when I came home from work Patty was taping up a photograph while Teddy sat at the table, and I asked what had been wrong with the last one, and Teddy, that son of a bitch, said to me, "Small dick," and then to *Patty*, "Of course, there is no man with a dick big enough for him." Some things about Teddy did not change.

As I think back over last year, some of my best, and sometimes funniest, memories are about our 23rd Psalm "rehearsals," as Teddy called them. They had started shortly after Teddy's return to the Pines. One night when I came home from work Teddy had a Bible on the coffee table with a classic-shaped martini glass on one side and a plate of tiny lobster rolls on the other (Teddy always did like theater) and when I had changed my clothes Teddy sat me down, handed me a martini and the Bible, opened to the right place, and said, "Read!" I told him that the entire idea was completely morbid and I refused and he insisted and we argued, of course, and he finally won with a low blow, saying, "You won't grant a dying man his only wish?" I was disgusted and I read it all in a rush: "The lord is my shepherd I shall not want he maketh me to lie down in green pastures he leadeth me beside the still waters he restoreth my soul he leadeth me in the paths of righteousness for his name's sake yea though I walk through the valley of the shadow of death I will fear no evil for thou art with me thy rod and thy staff they comfort me thou preparest a table before me in the presence of mine enemies thou anointest my head with oil my cup runneth over surely goodness and mercy shall follow me all the days of my life and I will dwell in the house of the lord forever amen." "That's not funny," Teddy said, and he started to coach me. He would say a line and make me repeat it, sometimes several times, and then we would go on to the next line. It became quite a joke between us over the months. I would recite it with a peculiar emphasis on one word or another ("The Lord is my shep*herd*"), and Teddy would do it with completely different accents and sometimes we would act out the lines. One of the last times we rehearsed was shortly before Thanksgiving after Teddy got out of the hospital. I was tired and depressed and Teddy seemed depressed too and we sat watching some moronic television show without speaking to each other, and suddenly Teddy turned off the TV with the remote and stood up and started chasing imaginary animals around the room and hooking them with an imaginary crook, having great difficulty keeping them in an orderly flock and keeping the rams from mounting the ewes, and the whole scene was so funny I couldn't help laughing, and I joined in. We had great fun when we got to "Thou preparest a table before me in the presence of mine enemies: thou anointest my head with oil; my cup runneth over." We acted out the food on the table—geese, turkeys, buffalo, peacocks, Rocky Mountain oysters (we had a bullfight to kill the bull, with much elegant capework on both our parts, and then Teddy pantomimed doing something very nasty to me with a certain part of the bull's anatomy), artichokes, cauliflower, and much more—and we armed the enemies with everything from slingshots to ICBMs. At the end, ". . . and I will dwell in the house of the Lord forever," Teddy constructed a castle in the air with his hands, a castle with turrets and banners, a castle that stretched off in the distance as far as one could see, and then opened the door, bowed to a figure sitting on a throne, and lay at the figure's feet and pretended to sleep, and then I did the same and lay with my arms around my Teddy. It was *not* a sad moment, and it is one that I will always remember.

We celebrated Thanksgiving (it was only last year, although it seems so long ago) here with a quiet dinner with Wayne. Some other friends came later, but Teddy was very tired and went to bed by eight so the party did not last very long. In the same week my parents came for my birthday, bringing a cake with them, and we had a little party. No one wanted to say anything about Christmas because we didn't know if Teddy would live even that long, but as my parents were leaving Teddy said, "I'll see you in Maine," and both Mother and Dad said of course and kissed him on the cheek. After Thanksgiving week Teddy almost never left the house, and the week before Christmas I tried to convince him not to go, but he wouldn't be convinced, so we went, although he was very ill then. It was a quiet, tranquil holiday, and Teddy really did enjoy it. We had not told Grandmother exactly what was wrong with him because we didn't want her to be afraid of getting the disease herself, but Teddy told me later that one afternoon she had asked him and he had told her. It didn't seem to make any difference to her. Teddy spent most of his time lying on a couch near the Christmas tree, and Grandmother often sat in a chair near him and read aloud, which he enjoyed. I played the piano a little for them, and one evening after I played, Grandmother said something about Grandfather and I asked Teddy if he remembered reciting the Christmas story from the Bible that first Christmas we spent there. Teddy looked confused and I was sorry that I had asked him, and we were all silent, but then Teddy started to speak, and he slowly recited those beautiful verses so quietly it was difficult to hear him. When he was finished I had to leave the room. Mother sat beside him, holding his hand.

Teddy managed to hang on to life for three and a half more months, and those months, at the beginning of this year, are as a distant dream to me. Our friends were there, helping out, closing around us, protecting us, but I barely felt their presence; they were like adults known when you were a child and then remembered when you yourself are an adult: forms; caricatures of people. I played the piano often for Teddy then, and he usually asked to hear the *Kinderscenen* or the *Goldberg Variations,* and sometimes when I would play other things—often Gershwin or Rachmaninoff— he would say, "That's too loud," and I would think of Grandmother saying the same thing. I was sick a lot myself in Teddy's final months, but I thought it was because of the physical and emotional strain of caring for Teddy and I ignored it.

Death came to him the way he wanted it. In early April he began to run very high fevers, and his doctor put him in the hospital for a final time. All our friends came for short visits, but he seemed not to recognize them or to care that they were there. However, when I came into the room and said hello he would smile—an asymmetric smile because of that damage the disease was doing to his brain—and, although he rarely spoke, he would watch me and move his eyes when I moved. He was in great pain, which morphine didn't touch, but he never cried out. He died, not at night but in the middle of the afternoon, as gracefully as any man can die. His blood pressure had been dropping and not responding to medication and a doctor told me it would happen soon. Teddy knew, too. The doctor stood away, by the window, and I held Teddy's hand and he moved his fingers a little and tried to speak but could not. After a few minutes the doctor came back to the bed and gave Teddy a final injection of morphine and the prick of the needle brought him back a little and he said, so quietly that it was but a breath, "Good-bye," and he lost consciousness. I sat beside him and stroked his head as his breath became shallower and slower and I remembered that first night I saw him, my blond-haired fantasy, and I remembered how happy I had been and I remembered our years together and I remembered beautiful nights on the Island, nights of dancing, stars, love, and I was not aware that his breathing had stopped until a nurse tapped me on the shoulder, and then I bent down and kissed his eyes and said, "Good-bye Teddy," and left.

I did not cry. I walked home. I made the necessary phone calls: to the funeral home we had made arrangements with; to his mother; to my parents; to our friends. Wayne came over and spent the night and we stayed up very late talking about Teddy, but still I did not cry. Although I was totally exhausted I went to work the next day, and every day for the next week. I constantly thought of my promise to Teddy to recite that damned Psalm, but I could not do it. Wayne spent a lot of time with me that week, and that Thursday night he told me that he was taking me to the Pines for the weekend. I said no, I wouldn't go, but Wayne told me I would be doing him a favor because he needed help opening the house, which had not been used since the previous

October, and he needed me to bring things out in my car. I knew it was just an excuse, a ruse to get me away, to force me to be comforted, but I was drawn to the place that Teddy and I had loved so much as a moth is drawn into a flame, and I agreed.

The sky was dark with thick, roiling clouds when we left and even darker when we reached the ferry in the late afternoon. There were only a few people going over and we all sat together and talked as we crossed the bay, and then when I stepped onto the dock at the harbor grief hit me like a solid wall and I would not speak for fear that if I opened my mouth I would sob. I helped Wayne carry one load of things to the house, and then he took the wagon back for more while I made a fire. I found a bottle of some kind of sweet liqueur that had been a house gift several seasons earlier, and I drank a little from the bottle—it tasted like bad cough syrup— and then I did cry; I remembered a time during the War Years when Teddy had been on the Island and had been unable to find anything in the house to drink and had also drunk some kind of disgusting liqueur from the bottle, and I stood in front of the fire with my hands on my face and sobbed. My tears gradually stopped and I knew I had to keep my promise to Teddy, and before Wayne returned I poured a glassful of the liqueur and took it with me to the beach. I walked toward the west, past the Grove, past Sailors' Haven, thinking the words, and as I walked rain started and intensified, and when I turned back it was dark and raining hard and I could not see but followed the ocean. At some point I realized that I was still carrying the glass and I put it down and continued on, exhausted, crying, stumbling in the heavy, wet sand, not knowing where I was. Eventually I reached the beginning of the Pines and the rain lightened and a few of the houses had lights burning in them, and as I walked I said that Psalm aloud, but very quietly, and I repeated it again and again, louder and louder, until I was opposite the steps that led to Wayne's house, and I stood at the edge of the roaring sea and screamed it out at the void, sobbing.

Chapter 8

Teddy had been right: The needles are awful. There are endless tests that require you to be pricked and probed, often by rough, uncaring, fearful nurses; there are long IV needles that often have to be placed into a new, fresh vein; there are frightening-looking needles for taking samples of spinal fluid, bone marrow, a few cells from your liver, arterial blood. You sleep badly with an IV needle in your arm and become exhausted to the point where every new puncture becomes an enervating ordeal. You are a pariah, and the mental effort it takes to maintain your dignity and self-possession while being treated like a dangerous animal is even more exhausting. You become accustomed to orderlies, janitors, others, working in your room as though you were not there and not responding when you speak to them. When you are strong enough you hang your IV bottle from a pole with wheels and shuffle through the halls, counting the tables holding gloves, masks, and gowns, knowing each table represents one more person with AIDS. You feel as though you are not living in reality, as though you are living in a slow-moving, inescapable dream, and you remember your life and wish you could change it and sometimes you think of suicide to protect your family and friends from the coming ordeal but you know you cannot protect them from the inevitable grief at the end, and sometimes you think again and again in an unstoppable litany, I do not want to die I do not want to die I do not want to die.

It was three weeks to the day after Teddy died that I found myself in the hospital with PCP. I had gotten a bad cold after that night on Fire Island and a week later I was coughing hard and running high fevers, and still I didn't know what was wrong; I thought I was just exhausted from Teddy's death. At first, AIDS did not occur to me. When I finally went to my doctor I could barely walk up the steps that led to his door, and thirty minutes after I went in to see him I was on my way to the hospital in a cab, shocked, numb. I was there for almost four weeks that first time, and then three weeks more not long ago. After I got out the first time, Blond Boy Alex took me home and when I came in I almost expected to find Teddy there, but of course he wasn't. He was gone.

Forever.

The first few weeks were hard because I was both understanding the reality of Teddy's death and beginning to understand the inevitability of my own, and I spent those weeks alternately in deep, suicidal depression and in periods of rage so intense that when they were over I could remember their existence but not what I had thought, or even what I had done. I came into the kitchen one morning and found it littered with broken china and shards of glass, but I remembered the night before as though someone else had been throwing things against the wall, not I, and I could not remember the sound that they must have made; I remembered them breaking in silent slow motion. I awoke from ragged sleeps screaming at Teddy and so wet with sweat that I had to change the sheets. I often cried.

When I was stronger I began to go out at night seeking companionship and, again, sex. The sex I had was very safe, but for a few weeks I could not get enough, and sought situations in which I was abused, hurt. I went to gay porno theaters and when I saw perfect, muscular young men having sex with each other on the screen it seemed as though I was living in a different time, separated from the world and from reality by my illness. I had lost much weight and my own body was no longer hard and strong but thin and weak and when I watched pornography I felt as though I were watching myself in the past, and I wanted to go back, to be young and hot and *physical,* to feel the sweat after a good run, to feel my arms and legs stretching against a cliff as I thought about how I would get to the next hold above, to feel that wonderful feeling of being in the water, drifting, sweating and exhausted, after a hard swim. It was these times, when I thought about how I once had been, that I sought, and found, rough, hard sex, and always I would not see my partner but would shut my eyes and see Teddy and see myself in the past.

I know it is irrational, but I was very angry with Teddy, not for giving me AIDS—I don't think he did— but because I needed him so much and he *died* on me when I needed him most. I remember one night a few months ago when Alex was here—he comes almost every day now—we were talking about Teddy and I pounded my fist on the table so hard I upset Alex's wineglass (I no longer drank) and yelled, "Why did I have to love *him!*", and Alex said, "We do not choose whom we love, whether it's a man or a woman, or even if we love at all. Our only choice is to reject it and be miserable or accept it and enjoy it as much as we can." "What about someone who doesn't love you back?" I asked, not thinking about Teddy but just about in general. "Ah, yes," Alex said in his best Shakespearean voice, "Unrequited love: simultaneously the most powerful, the most *beautiful*, feeling a person can have and the greatest torture." We spent the entire evening talking about love—gay love—and relationships, and Alex said that perhaps one thing the existence of AIDS will do is make gay life more oriented toward long-term relationships, that finally perhaps we will be able to enjoy some of the benefits of long-term stability that heterosexuals enjoy, which is not to say that many of us have not had stability, but only that even if we have we have not shared equally in its benefits: All legal benefits available to straight married couples are denied to us and to our lovers. Now, it is anathema to me that this horrible disease should have any benefits. I will not admit that it might be so, and I told Alex that night that it will be for historians to decide, and I am glad that I will not be around for the analysis. It was because of that conversation with Alex that I began to write this. Alex suggested that I write about Teddy and I started out by doing that, but then I decided to make it an autobiography, a story of just one gay man who enjoyed life, who enjoyed being gay, who loved his lover as much as one man can love another, and who will die before he is thirty.

I guess I really only had sex about a dozen times after I got out of the hospital before I stopped, for good. It was, as I have said, safe, very safe, and usually my partner knew about my illness, but as I began to live more easily with the knowledge that I was dying I began to feel guilty about what I was doing, and one night I made a careful, deliberate decision not to do it again. The knowledge that I would never again in my life experience sexual ecstasy, would never again be held securely by a powerful man while my heart beat in my temples and my breath came in gasps, made me very depressed and that night I sat on my fire escape for hours, thinking about jumping, until finally, when I was cold, I came back inside and threw out everything in the apartment that was connected with sex. Porno tapes, magazines, books, photographs of beautiful, naked men, tit clamps, dildoes, lubricant, rubbers, plastic gloves, handcuffs, leather, red bandannas: they all went into a large garbage bag that I then took downstairs and put outside on the curb. The next morning when I went out to get the paper I saw that the bag had been opened and most of its contents taken; the wind riffled the pages of a magazine and a dildo lay in the gutter. Videotape pulled from a cassette lay in ribbons on the sidewalk. I was terribly sad.

I began to feel very sorry for myself and wherever I went, whatever I did, the phrase *I don't deserve to die* ran around in my head and I could not escape it. Sometimes I would pound my fists on a table or against a wall and scream it through tears, and sometimes it would penetrate my sleep and jerk me into sudden consciousness, gasping, sweating. One night when this happened I got up—it must have been three or four in the morning—and sat at the piano without turning on any lights. I had not played at all for several weeks and at first I did not play but just looked at the keys, indistinct in the soft moonlight, and then I ran a finger up the keyboard in a slow, quiet glissando and sat in silence again for a while and then began to play, very slowly, the little Chopin Waltz in C-sharp Minor that I had first played when I was young. I remembered it well and it came easier and easier and gradually I accelerated and at the end I was playing it very quickly, too quickly for a performance, and so lightly my fingers just touched the keys, and when I was finished I was astonished that I had played so well.

A lot changed that night. My depression, my anger, began to recede, leaving in their place a tranquility that I still have. The next day I spent several hours playing the piano, with rest breaks of course, and as I played the memories that are set out on these pages began to flow in a steady, unstoppable stream, not chronologically but rather connected by themes—music, physicalness, location, sex, love—that were held together by the music. I have been surrounded by friends since I became ill, but until that day I had kept myself mentally apart from them, using my grief, my anger, my fear (I know now that I *was* afraid, although I didn't admit it to myself at first, and that fear is often with me), as a barrier, but that afternoon my cousin, Dick of Death Daniel, came over, and I was glad to see him and we sat on the couch and talked about, as we said, old times, and I asked him if he remembered the time I had grabbed his cock after Thanksgiving dinner. "You know," he said, "you have a one-track mind." "That's right," I said, and I leaned over and gave his crotch a good squeeze. It was *bigger* than I remembered. "*That* is impressive," I said, and Daniel laughed and pushed me away but then pulled me back, grabbed my crotch, and said, "*That* isn't," and kissed me on the cheek. Now, I've got a good eight inches, but Daniel was right, next to his it was not impressive. He and I talked for a while longer and then he left and later, when I was alone, I thought about Teddy and I missed him and I sat at my desk with a pad and a pen and began to write.

It's cooler now. I always thought that New York was at its most beautiful in late September, and this year it has been extraordinary. I went to the park this afternoon with John and Patty (Teddy called them Pussy Sniffer John and Saint Patricia), taking a cab to 72nd Street and then walking to Sheep Meadow, and I was almost amused to find myself walking like an old man and I did not reject the support John offered. When we reached the meadow I watched two shirtless youths, both short, brown, and muscular, passing a soccer ball between them and the sight of the outline of one of their penises made me smile. After I watched them play for a while I spread my jacket on the grass and lay back on it and looked at the clouds passing by in stately order, and gradually I fell asleep to the sounds of the kicking and bumping of the soccer ball and the calls of the young men using it, and just before I slept I wished that death could be like that: falling asleep on spicy-smelling grass with the warm sun on my face while nearby life, youth, vitality, live on.

I have probably had more visitors in the last few months than I had for the entire rest of my adult life. My parents come often (they want me to move home but I'm staying here), a GMHC volunteer comes two or three times a week, John or Patty or John and Patty stop in every day to see if they can run any errands for me, and my gay friends have been wonderful. I know a lot of people, and from the first week I was ill the cards, letters, phone calls, visits, flowers, have not stopped. And yet, still I feel very alone; I miss Teddy, and I admit that I'm afraid, although I haven't told anybody but Wayne. We talked about it a couple of weeks ago, and I told him that the worst thing about this mess is that Teddy went first so I'll have to go alone, and Wayne said he'd be there for me, but it's not the same; he's not Teddy.

I wore Teddy's black bomber jacket last week, the one he was wearing when I met him. Wayne invited Mother and Dad and me to his house in the Pines, and at first I didn't want to go because I thought that I might cry or somehow make a fool of myself, but Mother and Dad, probably in collusion with Wayne, said that they'd always wanted to see the Pines but wouldn't go without me, so, reluctantly, I said okay, knowing it

might be my last visit. Mother and Dad came here before we all left and they told me to take a jacket, and
when I opened the closet and saw Teddy's I had to
bring that. Can you imagine a gay pajama party with
your parents in attendance? That's what the weekend
was like. It was one of the last weekends of the season
and the weather was beautiful so everyone who'd been
in the house all summer was there. Wayne cleared out
a bedroom for my parents and put me in his bed and
everyone who was displaced slept on the couches in the
living room. We arrived Friday evening and I was tired
and went to bed early, but Mother went dancing with
some of the guys in the house and was out, I hear,
almost until dawn, and when she finally emerged from
the bedroom, sometime near noon, she said that she'd
never had a better time in her life. When I came into
the living area to go to the kitchen she was eating
breakfast with several of the housemates, who were
wearing only their underwear. (As I think I've said,
Mother has been called, by many, an incredible
woman.) Dad was amused by the whole thing and was
having a good time himself talking with the people in
the house and exploring the Island and walking on the
beach, but when Mother told him that he was going to
go dancing on Saturday night he said no he wasn't, and
Mother said fine, he was making dinner.

It was a perfect September day, cool, really too cool
for the beach although, of course, some hearty exhibi-
tionists were out there in their tight Speedos, and I

walked to the steps over the dunes and sat by myself
and watched the sea come in to the shore as it has
forever, and I thought about dying, but it was not as
much fear as curiosity. I took a nap later in the afternoon and probably would have slept through the night
except that Wayne woke me to ask if I wanted to go to
Tea. I really didn't want to go because I was afraid I'd
miss Teddy so much that I'd cry, but everyone in the
house was going, even my parents, and when at first I
said I was staying home Mother said gently, not as a
rebuke but as an old joke between friends, "Now don't
mope," and we smiled at each other and each remembered earlier, happier times, and I shook my finger at
her and laughed and put on my shoes. Wayne's house
is not too far from the Pavilion, so the walk wasn't too
hard, but when I got there I was tired and I sat with
Mother at a table while Wayne led my father around
and introduced him to some of our friends. Many people came to the table to say hello and I introduced them
to Mother and as I saw people saying good-bye for the
season I thought I knew how Teddy had felt when he
had said his own good-byes a year earlier—not sad, not
afraid, but feeling that things were coming to an end.
Dad did cook dinner that night, which we ate only in
candlelight, the light from the fire in the fireplace, and
the moonlight coming through the windows, and after
dinner Dad asked me if I felt like taking a walk and,
although I was really too tired to, I said yes. It was
quite cool by then, so I wore Teddy's jacket, and Dad

and I walked slowly, arm-in-arm, to the beach, and for the first time we talked about dying and about what I want done after I die. Our conversation had a feeling of great finality to it, as if it was the last serious one we would have, and as we sat on the steps watching the waves in the dim white moonlight I told Dad what a great father he'd been and that I was lucky to have had him and he told me that I was a wonderful son. We were quiet for a while and then Dad started to cry, and I put both arms around him and held him as tightly as I could and he lay his head on my shoulder and sobbed. Gradually his tears stopped and he dried his eyes and took my hand tightly in his and we walked slowly back to the house in silence.

My life now has become memories: memories of my youth, memories of Teddy, memories of things done only a year or two or a month or two ago all ebb and flow together, sometimes difficult to reclaim and sometimes surging up in great waves, and always changing. I find that as I look back over these pages now, after writing them, I remember some things differently than I did only a few months ago, and the earlier, recorded memory seems like a fiction while the current memory has the feel of truth. My days are filled with music. I don't play very much anymore, but instead listen to recordings; sometimes I listen to recordings of great pianistic war-horses and find joy in the sweep of the music and it keeps me in the present, but sometimes, when I have been sitting in silence for a while, before I write I sit at the piano and play a little Chopin or part of the *Kinderscenen* or some of the slower variations in the *Goldberg Variations* or the slower parts of the *Symphonic Etudes,* and when I do I live only in memory. Today when I played a few of the *Variations* I remembered the first time I tried to play them, the evening I told Dad I was gay, and when I thought about Dad I remembered when he first tried to teach me to swim and I do remember what happened; I did not make it to shore but started to sink and Dad lifted me out of the water and held me against his strong chest with my head on his shoulder and patted my back. I remember Grandfather swimming, wearing a long bathing suit that must have been fifty years old. Dad bought him a new one for Christmas once and Grandfather said he'd never wear it and told Dad to take it back. I remember Christmases in Maine when I was young, bouncing with excitement in the car on the way up, the confusion, the gifts, my grandparents quarreling. I remember now that the first time another man touched me sexually was one summer in Maine when I was, I think, thirteen; I was lying on a rock masturbating after a naked swim and a man, probably in his forties, came out of the woods and put his hand over mine and then pushed my hand away, and I remember that I was excited by his touch. I remember the night I met Teddy in the back room of a bar; instead of the customary interrogatory brush with one's fingers or the back of one's hand, he grabbed my crotch hard and didn't let go. I remember Teddy. The way he looked. Spoke. Walked. The way he made love. The way his muscles felt under my hands. I remember how strong he was. I remember when he was so weak too, in the hospital, when he could barely hold my hand. His room was always filled with flowers. I remember when he filled this apartment with flowers and candlelight for me. I remember walking out into my parents' garden when I was young and lying with my head in the irises, looking up at the blue sky through the blue petals. I remember what it felt like to be well. To be strong, when my body was lean and hard. I remember

Andrew John Ellis
Banker, 28

Andrew John Ellis, known to his many friends as A.J., died October 29 at New York University Medical Center of complications related to AIDS. He was 28 years old. An investment banker, Andrew was a familiar figure on the gay scene in New York and on Fire Island and was much loved by everyone who knew him. He was born in Greenwich, Connecticut, and received undergraduate and graduate degrees from Columbia University. Andrew is survived by his parents, Mr. and Mrs. Johnathon Ellis of Greenwich. His lover, Ted Erikson, died of AIDS-related complications this past spring. At Andrew's request, there were no services. Donations in his memory may be made to the People With AIDS Coalition.